Praise for
Mr. Bambuckle: Rule the School

"A male Mary Poppins of education, Mr. Bambuckle is every student's dream teacher."

—*Kirkus Reviews*

"A light and funny book, perfect for young readers."

—*Booklist*

"An original and credible cast of young characters and an ingenious, perspicacious adult protagonist… Harris balances outlandish classroom antics with students' heartfelt first-person stories…"

—*Publisher's Weekly*

"Mr. Bambuckle is an extraordinary teacher, and this is an extraordinary book."

—*Sunday Telegraph*

MR. BAMBUCKLE

Class 12B Goes Wild

TIM HARRIS

ILLUSTRATED BY
JAMES HART

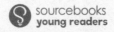

sourcebooks
young readers

First published in the United States in 2019 by Sourcebooks
Copyright © 2018, 2019 by Tim Harris
Cover and internal design © 2019 by Sourcebooks
Cover art by James Hart
Illustrations © 2018, 2019 by James Hart

Published by Sourcebooks Young Readers, an imprint of Sourcebooks Kids
P.O. Box 4410, Naperville, Illinois 60567-4410
(630) 961-3900
sourcebookskids.com

Originally published in 2018 as *Mr Bambuckle's Remarkables Go Wild* in Australia by Random House Australia Children's, an imprint of Penguin Random House Australia. This edition issued based on the paperback edition published in 2018 in Australia by Random House Australia Children's, an imprint of Penguin Random House Australia.

Library of Congress Cataloging-in-Publication Data

Names: Harris, Tim, author. | Hart, James (Illustrator), illustrator.
Title: Mr. Bambuckle : class 12B goes wild / Tim Harris ; illustrated by
   James Hart.
Other titles: Mr. Bambuckle's Remarkables go wild | Class 12B goes wild
Description: Naperville, IL : Sourcebooks Young Readers, 2019. | "Originally
   published in 2018 as Mr Bambuckle's Remarkables Go Wild in Australia by
   Random House Australia Children's, an imprint of Penguin Random House
   Australia." | Summary: "The class in room 12B are having fun in the
   wilderness. Until Miss Frost crashes camp!"-- Provided by publisher.
Identifiers: LCCN 2019021728 | (trade pbk. : alk. paper)
Subjects: | CYAC: Camping--Fiction. | School field trips--Fiction. |
   Teachers--Fiction. | Eccentrics and eccentricities--Fiction. |
   Behavior--Fiction. | Humorous stories.
Classification: LCC PZ7.1.H3748 Mv 2019 | DDC [Fic]--dc23 LC record available at https://lccn.loc.
gov/2019021728

Source of Production: Berryville Graphics, Inc., Berryville, VA, USA.
Date of Production: July 2019
Run Number: 5015682

Printed and bound in the United States of America.
BVG 10 9 8 7 6 5 4 3 2 1

FOR PAUL AND BETH,

two remarkable booksellers

The Students of Room 12B

EVIE NIGHTINGALE

Likes bright lights, open spaces, hugs

Dislikes being scared, basements, washing machines

SCARLETT GEEVES

Likes editing photos, asking questions, her favorite red ribbon

Dislikes too much cheese on pizza

SAMMY BAMFORD

Likes sports, skydiving, passing notes

Dislikes typos, the government, getting into trouble

VICTORIA GOLDENHORN

likes school, friends, music, sports, stickers

Dislikes none

HAROLD MCHAGIL

likes cricket, books by Tim Harris

Dislikes kilt dances, haggis, being embarrassed by his parents

SLUGGER CHOPPERS

likes breaking things, smashing things, destroying things, gourmet food

Dislikes fixing things

MIFFY "BIFFY" ARMSTRONG

likes being stronger than everybody else, activewear

Dislikes vegetables, math

DAMON DUNST

 likes Victoria Goldenhorn, photos of Victoria Goldenhorn, thinking about Victoria Goldenhorn

Dislikes anything without Victoria Goldenhorn

REN RIVERA

likes detecting, spying, living next door to Vinnie

Dislikes teachers who whisper in huddles

VINNIE WHITE

likes curling her hair, surprises, living next door to Ren

Dislikes homework

ALBERT SMITHERS

likes applied physics, chemical engineering, incredibly difficult math books

Dislikes lack of cheese on pizza

CARROT GRIGSON

Likes
living with Pop, feeding his pet pigeon

Dislikes
annoying ads on television

MYRA KUMAR

Likes
telling jokes, the internet, making money

Dislikes
boring people

VEX VRON

Likes
cars

Dislikes
almost everything except cars

PETER STRAYER (ABSENT)

Likes
absent on day of survey

Dislikes
absent on day of survey

1

Birds and Buses

The yellow bus rolled away from Blue Valley School with an air of excitement. Its driver, the much-loved Mr. Bambuckle, whistled a tune that matched the sparkle of his blue suit. While it was usual for the children to be taken away on a yearly camping trip, it was completely unusual that they knew nothing of this year's destination. In this case, Mr. Bambuckle had been arranging the surprise for quite some time.

"Do kindly close your eyes," said the charismatic teacher, "for we will soon approach a section of the journey you mustn't see."

The fifteen children obeyed without the slightest

delay. They had come to learn their teacher operated in remarkable ways, and this was something they were beginning to relish.

"You may now open your eyes, dear students," said Mr. Bambuckle.

"That was quick," said Sammy Bamford, straightening his baseball cap.

"Approximately nine seconds," said Albert Smithers, a blond-haired boy who wore glasses and liked to read a lot.

The bus passed beneath a stone bridge the children had never seen before. To the left wound a river, shimmering like diamonds in the afternoon sunlight. Thick forest lined the opposite bank.

"Where are we?" said Albert. "I've studied every map of the Blue Valley region, and there are no stone bridges."

Mr. Bambuckle grinned. "It's amazing what you miss when you close your eyes for nine seconds. Dodger chose this location especially, you know."

Only days before, the secluded campsite the bus now chugged toward had been discovered by a lively blue jay—Mr. Bambuckle's beloved pet, Dodger. The destination had been carefully selected to accommodate top secret schemes the teacher had been hatching.

"I can't believe you let a bird choose the campsite," said Miffy Armstrong.

"There's a good reason for it," explained the teacher. "Dodger has the ability to locate GPS black spots."

"GPS dreadlocks?" said Harold McHagil. "I'd like to see that."

"He said black spots, you funny bunny," said Scarlett Geeves with a chuckle.

"I'm confused," said Miffy. "What do GPS black spots have to do with anything?"

"My dear Miffy," said Mr. Bambuckle, "I would love to tell you more, but that would be taking away the fun of the chase. You'll figure it out when the time comes."

"The chase?" Miffy shrugged her shoulders, though

she could tell by her teacher's tone that he was plotting something quite extraordinary. It sent a tingle down her spine, and as far as tingles go, this one was particularly delicious.

The bus slowed down and turned left, bumping over another stone bridge that crossed the river. The road straightened out and stretched deep into the forest. Albert adjusted his glasses and squinted outside, determined to find a landmark that sparked a map-reading memory.

The black asphalt soon turned to dirt, and the road curved around to the left, taking it back toward the river. The trees—tall and impressive—cast shadows that blinked over the windshield.

"I need someone to take the wheel for a moment," said Mr. Bambuckle. "Slugger, would you be so kind?"

Slugger Choppers, a bulky boy with arms as thick as the trees outside, lumbered to the front of the bus. "Me?"

"That's right, Slugger. I believe you have experience."

Slugger's mind flashed back to a few weeks earlier

when he had taken advantage of a government typo that allowed anyone older than eight the same rights as eighteen-year-olds. He had spent an entire day behind the wheel of a forty-two-seat bus. "Yeah, I can drive for you."

Mr. Bambuckle slid out from his seat and stood near the door while Slugger took control.

"What's happening?" said Evie Nightingale, a small girl who was easily frightened.

"I have an urgent matter to attend to," said Mr. Bambuckle. "Slugger, would you please?" He tapped the door.

"Open it?" said Slugger.

"That's right."

Slugger shrugged and pressed a button on the dash. Wipers suddenly swished across the windshield. "Oops."

He tried another control.

Yeah, yeah, yeah, baby, you make my heart go wiiild.

"That's the radio, Slugger," said Mr. Bambuckle.

Slugger's meaty fists fumbled over the dashboard

as he punched yet another button. The toilet at the back of the bus flushed loudly. "I'll get it in a minute," he apologized.

"Try the orange switch," said the teacher patiently.

The door swung open, and Mr. Bambuckle stepped out of the moving vehicle.

The students gasped.

"Is he okay?"

"I can't see him!"

"Where did he go?"

"Did we run over him?"

Before they had time to fully register what had happened, Mr. Bambuckle stepped back onto the bus—seemingly out of thin air. "All is well, dear children. It appears Dodger had flown into some difficulty."

The blue jay fluttered its wings, perched on the teacher's shoulder. He chirped sweetly.

"Dodger!" cried Sammy. "Is he all right, Mr. Bambuckle?"

The teacher nodded. "Yes, though the speckled-dagger vulture can be rather nasty this late in the afternoon. I managed to get there just in time."

Albert shot his hand up. "I've read over twenty-seven books about birds, and there's no such thing as a speckled-dagger vulture."

Vinnie White, a tall girl with curly brown hair, laughed. "Over twenty-seven books! What does that even mean?"

"Twenty-eight," said Albert. "And there is no such bird."

"That's because it hasn't been discovered yet," said Mr. Bambuckle.

While Albert would usually argue a point, he was beginning to trust his teacher's knowledge. "Oh," he said. "You learn something new every day."

Dodger fluttered off Mr. Bambuckle's shoulder and

looped around the inside of the bus. The students clapped as the blue jay performed some difficult spins and dives.

"He *really* is a beautiful bird," said Slugger, who usually reserved words like *beautiful* for cooking.

"He most certainly is," agreed Mr. Bambuckle. "And Slugger, keep an eye on the road, since you're no longer on it."

"Argh!"

The bus slammed to a halt, inches from a giant, twisted gum tree.

"We're very close to those branches," said Carrot.

"We're here!" announced Mr. Bambuckle. "Kindly unpack your belongings and set up your tents before dark."

The students stepped off the bus and into a clearing. The twisted gum, which stood impressively in the center of the small campsite, was surrounded by soft grass that carpeted the ground. To one side of the tree, about a dozen fallen logs formed a circle around what was clearly a fire pit. On the other side, a pebbly path led from the edge of the scrub to the river. The rest of the clearing was surrounded by deep-green forest. It was picturesque.

Once everyone was unpacked, Slugger reversed the bus back to the dirt road and parked it there.

"You're not just a talented cook," said Mr. Bambuckle. "Nice maneuver."

Slugger beamed, his cheeks flushing the color of sautéed radishes.

Damon Dunst approached the teacher, a sheepish look on his face. "Umm…sort of a problem…"

"I am always here to help," said Mr. Bambuckle. "Just tell me what it is."

Damon scratched the side of his head. "I kinda forgot to pack a tent."

How to Put Up a Tent

A REFLECTION BY DAMON DUNST

This guide is dedicated to the love of my life:
Victoria Goldenhorn.

♡ __Do:__ Remember to pack a tent.

☠ __Don't:__ Forget to pack a tent because you were so excited about camp.

♡ __Do:__ Thank the teacher, who brought a spare tent and has kindly given it to you.

☠ __Don't:__ Thank the teacher, then revel in the moment by drinking undiluted fruit punch concentrate.

♡ __Do:__ Stop drinking after half a cup.

☠ __Don't:__ Drink a full cup.

♡ **Do:** Stop drinking after a full cup.

☠ **Don't:** Continue drinking one, two, three, and four more cups.

♡ **Do:** Eat something bland to help counteract the sugar.

☠ **Don't:** Eat a packet of gummy bears and seven chocolate cookies because you're on a sugar roll.

♡ **Do:** Burp quietly and politely.

☠ **Don't:** Walk up to Victoria and say, "Hey, sorry to interrupt you while you're putting up your tent. I have something really important to tell you. I'm terribly regretful for disturbing you. I wouldn't do so if it wasn't urgent. It's just that... Well, you see... There's this thing, and I need to... BUUURRRP!"

♡ **Do:** Apologize.

☠ **Don't:** Follow up with an even bigger burp.

♡ **Do:** Walk away.

☠ **Don't:** Pretend you're a horse and gallop away, smacking your bottom and neighing at the top of your voice. (The sugar has kicked in.)

♡ <u>Do:</u> Sit down under a tree and wait for the sugar hit to wear off.

☠ <u>Don't:</u> Climb the tree because... Well, just because!

♡ <u>Do:</u> Hold tightly to the branches as you climb.

☠ <u>Don't:</u> Fall out of the tree because the sugar hit has tricked you into thinking you're Tarzan. (Swinging on vines is not as easy as it looks in the movies. Plus, Tarzan has more hair on his chest than you. Though not as much as Harold McHagil's father.)

♡ <u>Do:</u> Land on soft grass.

☠ <u>Don't:</u> Land on Slugger Choppers.

♡ <u>Do:</u> Let Slugger's angry fists startle you back to reality.

☠ <u>Don't:</u> Giggle at Slugger's hands because they smell like rosemary and paprika. (He truly is an expert in gourmet food.)

♡ <u>Do:</u> Calm down. (Try to calm Slugger down too. In his clumsy rage, he knocked over Sammy's tent.)

☠ <u>Don't:</u> Start daydreaming about Victoria.

♡ **Do:** Snap out of your daydream.

☠ **Don't:** Imagine that you've taken Victoria on a romantic rowboat ride down a sparkling river.

♡ **Do:** Gently paddle the boat through the lilies and make interesting conversation with your date.

☠ **Don't:** Rock the boat from side to side until it nearly flips over.

♡ **Do:** End the daydream now!

☠ **Don't:** Add raging rapids to the river so you can impress Victoria with your boating skills.

♡ **Do:** Steer away from the rocks.

☠ **Don't:** Slam into the rocks, capsizing the boat.

♡ **Do:** Reach for Victoria and pull her up from beneath the frothing waters.

☠ **Don't:** Start sinking because you can't swim.

♡ **Do:** Remember it's a daydream and you can swim.

☠ **Don't:** Remember it's a daydream and you can swim and there are ferocious crocodiles in the water.

♡ **Do:** Wrestle the crocodiles away from Victoria and pull her to the safety of the shore.

☠ **Don't:** Enjoy wrestling the crocodiles so much that it turns into a bizarre synchronized swimming event.

♡ **Do:** Stop. The. Daydream. Now.
☠ **Don't:** Add disco lights and a dance floor and boogie with the crocodiles.

♡ **Do:** Snap back to reality and get to the task at hand. Systematically unpack your tent and check that all the parts are there.
☠ **Don't:** Try to impress Victoria by being a helicopter and swinging the tent bag over your head, scattering parts across the grass.

♡ <u>Do:</u> Carefully gather the tent pieces and check nothing is astray.

☠ <u>Don't:</u> Challenge yourself to collect everything in less than twenty seconds and then miss one of the important poles that fell behind some bushes.

♡ <u>Do:</u> Unfold the main part of the tent, ensuring everything is the right way up. Peg down the edges.

☠ <u>Don't:</u> Peg down the edges before you discover the tent is upside down.

♡ <u>Do:</u> Take the pegs out of the ground and flip the tent the right way up.

☠ <u>Don't:</u> Try to flip the tent while it's still pegged down. (This will tear the canvas through the middle.)

♡ <u>Do:</u> Take the damaged tent back to the teacher and apologize profusely. Explain that you also lost one of the main poles.

☠ <u>Don't:</u> Take the damaged tent back to the teacher and apologize profusely, then ask if you can borrow a sleeping bag because you forgot to pack that too. Oh dear.

Around the Fire

The late afternoon sun was the color of golden syrup. Albert scrunched up several pieces of newspaper and placed them around the base of a woodpile. "It's ready for lighting, Mr. Bambuckle."

The teacher stepped forward, reaching deep into one of his pockets. "Kindly stand back, dear children. This can be rather dangerous." He bent down next to the pile of wood and cupped his hands, taking great care not to show the students what he held.

"It *must* be the Indian spark-maker beetle," whispered Victoria.

"The Indian spark-maker beetle!" echoed Sammy, his voice trembling with excitement.

Ever since the students in room 12B met Mr. Bambuckle, they had been pressing him about the mysterious insect. Whenever the subject was raised, however, the teacher dismissed it as being "too dangerous" or "incredibly deadly."

Mr. Bambuckle reached into an opening in the pile of wood. As he did, yellow sparks flew in several directions, setting the kindling alight. Flames soon licked the base of the woodpile, growing stronger by the second.

"Well," said the teacher, his hands still cupped, "that's *one* way to light a fire."

The students inched closer to Mr. Bambuckle. It was a moment they had been dreaming of.

"It's amazing," said Albert.

"Unbelievable," said Myra.

"Absolutely brilliant," whispered Harold.

"Can we see the beetle?" pleaded Victoria.

"What beetle?" said Mr. Bambuckle.

"The Indian spark-maker beetle—the one you used to light the fire."

"Oh," said the teacher, opening his hands for the children to see. "I used a match."

The students groaned, disappointed at the sight of the blackened stick.

"That reminds me," said Mr. Bambuckle. "Please don't ask to see my Indian spark-maker beetle, for it is extremely unsafe."

"Like the speckled-dagger vulture?" asked Albert.

"Far, far more dangerous, dear Albert."

The students sat down on the logs around the fire, admiring the flames against the darkening sky. Their faces glowed in the warmth.

Mr. Bambuckle glanced at a small gray tent away from the fire. Inside slept Vex Vron, a boy badly fatigued by too many late nights.

Vex had made a deal with his father, agreeing to work in one of the family's car dealerships after school. In exchange, his father had offered vehicle upgrades to members of Blue Valley's school board. The deal had guaranteed the return of Mr. Bambuckle to room 12B after he had been fired by Mr. Sternblast. While Vex was initially happy to make the sacrifice, the late nights had caught up with him. Hints of his rebellious nature had begun to resurface.

Vex's tent was pitched just far enough away from the others to ensure he couldn't be disturbed. The children were told this was simply to allow the troubled boy to sleep. Mr. Bambuckle, however, had a greater plan in mind for Vex. Sleep was only the beginning.

"Do you think Mr. Sternblast would allow a campfire?" asked Sammy.

"Probably not," said Albert. "He's always angry these days."

Mr. Sternblast had indeed been in fine form of late. Having recently missed out on a higher-paying job in the city, the principal had introduced a new discipline policy to help boost grades at Blue Valley. With the new policy came a new assistant principal—the ever-icy Miss Frost. Along with Mr. Sternblast, she was making life miserable for everyone.

Even Mr. Bambuckle was struggling against the tyranny of administration and procedures. He was working extra hard to ensure room 12B appeared to fall into line with the principal's demands, and he had enlisted the help of Dodger. The blue jay would fly into the room and chirrup a tune to warn the teacher if trouble was coming.

If Miss Frost was on her way, Mr. Bambuckle would clap his hands and say "Barnacle." This was the code word for his students. The children would rush madly around the room, shoving their experiments, models, novels, and projects into cupboards before racing back to their desks.

Dodger would give a final chirp and disappear into one of the inside pockets of Mr. Bambuckle's jacket.

Then, like clockwork, Miss Frost would step into the room and look around, her lips twitching as she searched for fault. "You there, Alfred, sit up straighter." Her whisper made the hairs on necks stand tall.

"It's Albert."

"It's detention. May I remind you not to talk back to me."

Mr. Bambuckle would stand at the front of the room and speak blandly about meaningless facts and figures and the importance of boosting grades. The students would nod and pretend to listen. Then, as soon as Miss Frost exited the room, they would breathe easy and return to their original projects.

Now, sitting around the fire, miles from the classroom, the children were beginning to unwind.

"Who would like a marshmallow?" said Mr. Bambuckle.

"Me, please!" chorused the class.

"First, you'll need to find something to cook them with."

The students eagerly melted into the woods, searching for the perfect roasting stick.

Carrot Grigson was the first to return, and he was panting.

"Are you okay?" asked Ren, who was the next back to the fire.

"*That* was weird."

"What was?"

Carrot gulped. "When I was looking for a stick, I heard this massive *whoosh* go past my head."

"How strange," said Ren, whipping out a notebook. "Can you give me more details?"

"It was a deep *whoosh*," said Carrot. "It sounded pretty big. But it was too dark to see clearly, so I ran back as fast as I could."

Ren scratched her head. "Beats me."

The rest of the class were now returning, and each student took a seat around the fire.

"Is this dinner?" asked Scarlett. "Are we only having marshmallows?"

"Goodness, no," said Mr. Bambuckle. "Our guest hasn't arrived yet."

Before the children had time to ask who the guest was, Mr. Bambuckle dipped his hand into one of his pockets, pulling out a plump bag of marshmallows. "Would someone kindly distribute these?"

Vinnie White was up in a flash. "I'll do it!" She opened the bag and began to move around the circle. One by one, her classmates attached a gooey sweet to the end of their sticks.

"Hey, Vinnie," teased Ren. "You'll do *anything* for marshmallows."

"Here we go," said Vinnie. "I bet you're going to tell the whole world about Aunt Agatha's marshmallow pie."

Ren giggled. "*You* should have the honor of telling *that* story."

"Stories are best told around campfires," said Mr. Bambuckle.

"What do you mean?" said Vinnie, sitting down next to Ren.

"What I mean, dear Vinnie, is we would be delighted to be your audience."

Vinnie's face broke into a grin. The entire class leaned forward, their marshmallows roasting slowly over the embers, as she began to tell her story.

The Suck-Up

Vinnie White's Story

I've always been a bit of a suck-up. I have this knack for being able to make adults give me what I want. Whether it be schoolteachers, athletic coaches, store clerks, or doctors, I was blessed with the gift of persuasion.

I've even had luck with Cafeteria Carol—no easy feat in anyone's books. Unless you're Mr. Bambuckle.

"Good morning, Carol," I said. "What a beautiful day it is."

"What do you want?" Carol's voice was flat and hostile.

I curtseyed and dipped my head. "You look stunning today. Have you done something with your hair?"

"I haven't touched my hair since 2013. What do you want?"

I looked through the menu and chose something healthy. "I'd like a bunch of grapes."

"Say 'please.'"

"Please, please, pleasey, o-please, o-please, o-please, pretty please, please, pleasey, pleasey, please, may I have some grapes, you beautiful woman, you."

Carol wiped her greasy fingers on her apron and plucked a bunch from the fruit bowl. "That's fifty cents," she said.

"Oh, thank you, thank you, thank you," I said, putting my money on the counter. I had exact change. "You're a national treasure."

Carol stared ahead without blinking. "You're a national pest. Next."

"There's just one more teeny-weeny thing," I said.

"Could I please, please, pretty please have an extra grape? I'll be your best friend."

Carol dropped her gaze without flinching. "An extra grape?"

"Only if your big, beautiful heart so wishes," I said.

She sighed and plunged her grubby hand into the fruit bowl, retrieving a single squashed grape. She plonked it onto the counter. There was a big thumbprint pressed into the center, and bits of juice had burst from one end. "Beat it," she said.

I snatched the grape and ran.

Yes, I became somewhat of a playground legend that day. Nobody gets free stuff from Cafeteria Carol. Well, nobody except Mr. Bambuckle, who somehow succeeded in scoring chocolate bars for the entire class. I have *no* idea how he managed *that*!

Some grown-ups are harder to persuade than others, mind you. Mrs. Wordsmith may have been a soft target when I was in her kindergarten class, but she has been onto me ever since she realized I had successfully sucked up through the entire first year of school.

I'll never forget my very first kindergarten spelling test. Mrs. Wordsmith stood at the front of the room and read out the words. "Number one—cat."

"Excuse me, Mrs. Wordsmith," I said in my sweetest voice.

"Yes, Vinnie?"

"Can you please give us a teeny-weeny clue?"

Mrs. Wordsmith smiled. "The first letter is *C*."

"You are the kindest lady in the whole wide room," I said.

A couple of kids giggled.

"Excuse me again," I said.

"Yes, Vinnie?"

"Can you please give us another itty-bitty clue?"

Mrs. Wordsmith was only too pleased to oblige. "The next letter is *A*."

"You are the kindest lady in the whole wide school."

Myra Kumar snorted with laughter.

"One last thing," I said.

"Yes, Vinnie?"

"Can you please give us just one more itsy-bitsy clue?"

The teacher chuckled. "The last letter is *T*."

"You are the kindest lady in the whole wide Blue Valley."

I managed to adorably extract every single letter of every single word that day. It was all too easy.

"Well done, Vinnie," said Mrs. Wordsmith, handing back my marked test. "You scored ten out of ten."

I batted my eyelashes. "You're the best."

Yes, sucking up to adults is all too easy.

Well, most of the time.

Aunt Agatha is the *one* grown-up I've never been able to crack. No matter what I try, no matter how much I suck up, she doesn't fall for it. It's like she has built-in bootlicking sensors.

She lives in a tiny house with her boyfriend, Ralph. He's almost ninety years old, but that's good for Aunt Agatha, because she's almost eighty.

Sometimes Mom and Dad send my brother, Justin, and me to stay with Aunt Agatha during the school breaks. Ralph doesn't enjoy the visits, because he values his privacy and complains about all the noise we make. I guess that's what you worry about when you're old.

Justin is a pretty decent older brother, but he's not very good at sucking up. "Aunt Agatha, may I please have a slice of your marshmallow pie?" he asked one day. Mom and Dad had gone on an overseas vacation, and we were staying for two weeks.

The pie sat steaming on the kitchen counter. It smelled like walking into a bakery first thing in the morning. The best part—the top of the pie—was smothered in glorious golden goop—dozens of hot marshmallows.

"No," said Aunt Agatha.

Justin's head drooped, and he trudged back up the squeaky hallway to his room.

I thought I'd try my luck. "Aunt Agatha, may *I* have a slice of the pie?"

"Not today, Vinnie. I'm taking this one to the bowling alley for a special occasion."

My mouth was watering like Niagara Falls. "*Please*, may I have a slice?"

"No."

"Pretty please?"

"No."

"Pretty, pretty please?"

"Still no."

"Pretty, pretty, pretty please with cherries on top?"

"They're not cherries. They're marshmallows. Go and get ready to come to the bowling alley."

I really should have walked away then. Aunt Agatha had made it perfectly clear she didn't care too much for my apple-polishing. But I was stubborn in my craving for suck-up power, and I desperately wanted a taste of the pie. "I'll be your best friend," I wheedled.

Aunt Agatha responded by placing the marshmallow pie on the top shelf in the kitchen cupboard. "No!"

A tiny spark—a fizz of determination—zipped through my body. I *had* to have some of that pie, and I wasn't going to stop until I got my way. "Okay, lovely Aunt Agatha, I understand." I twisted a curl of hair around my little finger. "I will obey your every command."

Ralph shuffled over to his car—a white, vintage Ford sedan—and popped the trunk open. He loaded it with flowers clipped fresh from the garden. I had to admit, they smelled divine.

"What's with the roses?" I asked.

Ralph huffed. "I'm doing something."

He didn't like being interrupted when he was "doing something." Which seemed to be always.

To amuse myself, I made a game of following him around the house and trying to get his attention, just for fun. No matter what I asked, it was always the same response.

"Sorry to bother you while you're watching television. I wondered if—"

"Not now. I'm doing something."

"May I read that magazine when you're done?"

"Go away. I'm doing something."

"May I have the saltshaker after you?"

"Be quiet. I'm doing something."

"I need to use the bathroom when you're out."

"Stop hounding me. I'm doing something."

That was something I'd rather him *not* be doing. But that's beside the point. The point is, I wanted some of the marshmallow pie.

Ralph returned to the house and wiped his shoes on the doormat. He always did that when he'd been in the garden.

Justin joined me at the car. "It must be Oldies Day at the alley or something," he said. "Aunt Agatha is putting on lipstick."

"Gross," I said. "There's nothing quite like wrinkly red kisses."

"Don't make me gag," said Justin. He pouted his lips. "I'm Aunt Agatha, and I'm in love with Ralph. Smoochie, smoochie, smoochie."

I cracked up.

Aunt Agatha walked out to the car. She was carrying the pie. "Out of the way, children, I need to put this on the front seat."

"Here, let me carry it for you," I said.

"Thank you, Vinnie, but I don't need your help."

I scooted around to the passenger side and opened the door. "But it's always such a pleasure to be of service," I said with a smile.

"You're not having any of the pie," said Aunt Agatha, catching on to my ploy. "It's for the special occasion. Besides, I have enough trouble keeping that pesky Cookie Simpson away from my desserts. That man's sweet tooth is notorious for making cakes and pastries disappear in the blink of an eye. I don't want you to turn into a sweets scavenger like him." She brushed past me and placed the pie on the seat.

"What *is* the special occasion?" said Justin. "You and Ralph have been awfully quiet about it all."

Aunt Agatha shook her head. "It's a surprise. You'll find out when we get there. Now, you kids wait here a few more minutes while Ralph and I get the final things ready."

"Yes, Aunt Agatha."

I peered through the passenger window at the pie on the front seat. The marshmallows were tantalizing me with their golden glow. "It's killing me," I said. "I *need* that pie."

"No chance," said Justin. "You heard Aunt Agatha. It's for the special occasion."

"I know how to make her crack," I said. "She hasn't seen the best of me yet."

I crept down the side of the house to the shed in

the backyard. It's where Ralph keeps his tools and work things—a near century of workman life wrapped in corrugated tin.

The shelves and tables were crammed with odds and ends. There were glass jars filled with nails, piles of sandpaper, hammers, drills, scraps of wood, and ice cream containers labeled with masking tape. I spotted what I was after and swiped it from the shelf. Aunt Agatha and Ralph would be so pleased with me. They'd *have* to let me try the pie after this.

Justin eyed me suspiciously when I returned to the car. "What are you up to?"

"It *is* a special occasion," I said. "So I'm going to polish the car for them. They'll love me for it!"

The can of polish was easy to open, because the lid was on crooked. I'd seen Dad do it before by wedging his nails in the gap. The lid popped off and rattled to the ground.

"It smells more like a new house than car polish," said Justin.

I ignored him, dipped a cloth into the polish, and started to rub it all over the white hood. It left a purple streak, but I remembered watching Dad polish our car. There were always smears that needed to be rubbed in. So I rubbed harder.

Justin leaned over the hood. "Are you sure this is polish?"

"Pretty sure," I said, rubbing faster and faster. The hood was slowly turning violet.

"*Pretty* sure?" said Justin. "As opposed to *definitely* sure?" He bent down and picked up the container. "Vinnie, stop!"

Aunt Agatha and Ralph rushed outside as fast as old people can. Which is actually quite slow. They gave me just enough time to start polishing the side of the car too. Well, both sides. And maybe a little bit of the trunk. And perhaps a tire or two. Do you even polish wheels? Well, I gave it a try.

"Stop at once, you wicked child!" snapped Aunt Agatha.

"I tried to make her stop," said Justin. "But she wouldn't listen."

The once-white car flaunted its patchy purple jacket on the driveway. There were streaks of violet—some gloopier than others—stained across the front, sides, back, and wheels.

Ralph's cheeks were blooming patches of red. "What have you done to my Ford!?"

☆☆☆

I stared out the window as we pulled up at traffic lights. Justin couldn't see out of his, because it was coated in purple paint.

"In all my years, I've never seen anything like it," fumed Aunt Agatha. She was holding the pie on her lap. "And on the day of our special occasion."

"I'm sorry," I said. "I was only trying to help. Truly."

"You need to learn how to spell," said Justin. "*Purple* and *polish* are two very different words."

"They both start with *P*," I said. I thought back to all

my spelling lessons in kindergarten. Maybe I should have paid more attention to Mrs. Wordsmith instead of sucking up for the answers.

The car continued crawling through traffic on its way to the bowling alley. I had messed up. Was I losing my touch? It *was* an accident.

We eventually pulled in front of the bowling alley and were met with stares of bewilderment from the other guests and patrons.

Aunt Agatha's face softened a little at the sight of her friends. "Now, let's just forget that whole incident. We're here to celebrate."

I hastily unclicked my seat belt, opened the door, and dashed around to the passenger side. "Here, let me take the pie for you," I said.

To my surprise, Aunt Agatha let me lift it off her lap. The dense weight of deliciousness almost knocked me over. "Wow, it's heavy," I said. "May I please try some? It'll make it lighter to carry."

"You're turning into an even bigger dessert vulture than Cookie Simpson," said Aunt Agatha. "And that's saying something. He's a pudding pest!" She stepped out of the car and relieved me of the pie. "The answer is still no."

Just before we reached the entrance, Aunt Agatha turned to face me and Justin. "This is a very important event for us, so make sure you behave. I've packed you both cheese sandwiches. You are *not* to touch the pie. Or any of the other food for that matter."

"I promise I won't touch any food," I said.

Though I'm not sure I meant it.

☆ ☆ ☆

The bowling alley was filled with seniors dressed in their Sunday best. There was a live band performing in the corner, also made up of retired people. It looked like they were playing in slow motion. I've never seen hair grow out of a drummer's ears faster than he can hit the snare drum.

The marshmallow pie was the showpiece on a table

already overflowing with sweets and cakes. There were pastries and shortbreads, muffins and pies, as well as a thousand caramel donuts. The other guests had gone to a great deal of effort to cater for the occasion.

"I badly want to try some of the pie," I said.

Justin rolled his eyes. "Here we go again. Didn't you learn your lesson with the car? You can't just have what you want all the time."

Ignoring my brother, I walked over to Aunt Agatha. She was dancing with Ralph (in slow motion) and looked like she was having a good time.

I tugged on her dress. "I just want to say that your dancing is heavenly."

Aunt Agatha's built-in bootlicking sensors were on high alert. She tilted her head as if to say "go away."

"Is there anything I can do for you? You know, to help in any way?"

She frowned. "How about buying Ralph a new car?"

Not a bad idea if I had enough money. Maybe Ralph

could hire me to do some errands. I could start by unpol-
ishing his Ford.

I tapped him on the elbow. "Is there anything I can
do for *you*?"

Ralph grunted and pulled away from Aunt Agatha.
"Go away. I'm doing something."

Typical. Was it the only excuse he had?

As fate would have it, Ralph was really doing
something this time. I mean, *really* doing
something—something unfathom-
ably huge.

He got down on one
knee—which took such a
long time, the band got
through two and a half
more songs—and pulled a
small box from his pocket.
Everyone became
silent and formed

a ring around the couple. It was as though they had all known this moment was coming.

"You know how much I love you," said Ralph, gazing up at Aunt Agatha. "Would you do me the honor of marrying me?"

The crowd erupted into cheers at Aunt Agatha's enthusiastic nods. The elderly lovers were engaged.

"Mom and Dad are in for a shock when they get home," said Justin.

Aunt Agatha tapped a microphone. "Thank you all for joining us," she said. "It's lovely to celebrate our engagement with you. Everyone here means a lot to us. You're like family."

The guests clapped.

"I'm not one for lengthy speeches," continued Aunt Agatha. "I say it's time we eat!" She shot me a fierce look, reminding me my only choice was cheese sandwiches.

Ralph tottered over to the food table and picked up

the marshmallow pie, showing it off to the crowd. "She's a clever girl, my Agatha. Baked this earlier today."

The goodness of the pie was too much, and my desire to eat it was too strong. Now was my moment.

"Here, let me help you serve it up," I said, skipping over to the food table.

"Vinnie," warned Aunt Agatha, "we spoke about this."

"Don't do it," said Justin.

"Let me help," I said to Ralph.

"Not now. I'm doing something."

"You're *always* doing something," I said. "Let me take the pie."

"Get lost."

"Please?"

"No."

"Pretty please?"

"No."

"I'll be your best friend."

"NO!"

I grabbed the edge of the plate the pie was on. "Just. Let. Me. Take. It."

Ralph was strong for an almost-ninety-year-old. He wrestled it out of my hands. "Buzz off. I'm doing something."

Then another pair of hands latched onto the plate, tugging it out of Ralph's grasp. "The pie is mine!"

An old man—dressed in suspenders, short shorts, and high socks—gripped the plate so tightly, his bony knuckles went as white as his wispy hair.

"Who are *you*?" I said.

"Cookie Simpson," he cackled. "And this pie is mine!"

Ralph grabbed hold of the plate and pulled it hard toward him.

Cookie didn't let go, yanking it back.

The old men wrestled and wrangled and heaved and hauled. Neither of them were going to let go of the pie.

"Hands off!" yelled Ralph.

"I will not surrender!" bellowed Cookie.

The plate began to tilt toward the floor.

Ralph mustered all his strength and gave an enormous tug. Cookie's hands slipped from the plate, and he crashed backward into the table, catapulting desserts across the room. They flew over the heads of the guests like sugary cannonballs, landing with loud plops on the floor.

"Fiddlesticks!" Ralph stumbled sideways into me. He flung out an arm and grabbed my shoulder to steady himself, losing control of the precious plate. The pie did a triple backflip, almost in slow motion, and tumbled to the floor.

"Nooo!" I called, diving forward with both arms outstretched.

I managed to catch the plate inches from the ground, my elbows burning as I slid across the carpet.

Silence.

Aunt Agatha was mortified. She raced over to check on Ralph and glared at Cookie, who was by now looking a little sheepish, even if he was busy drooling over the spilled desserts on the floor.

The pie felt warm in my hands. The marshmallows on top had somehow stayed perfectly intact. I could reach out and take a bite if I wanted. Nobody could stop me.

But could I stop myself?

A pleasant feeling washed over me like melted butter on toast as the thought sunk in. I *could* stop myself.

I stood up and carefully passed the pie to Aunt Agatha. "Congratulations on your engagement to Ralph," I said quietly. "I'm sure you'll enjoy the pie."

Aunt Agatha's face turned as soft as a marshmallow. "Thank you, Vinnie," she said. "You have shown enormous discipline to give it back."

I smiled. It felt good to have some self-control.

A slopping noise disrupted the moment. Cookie Simpson was on his hands and knees, gobbling one of the splattered caramel donuts on the floor. He slurped and slobbered, lapping up the mess like a vacuum.

"Now *that*," I said, admiring a master in action, "is how to suck up."

3

Snap

A sense of pride filled Vinnie as she finished telling her story. It was the first time she had spoken at length to a group this large. "Thanks for listening, guys," she said.

Mr. Bambuckle took the last marshmallow out of the bag. "I'm certain everyone would agree with me that you'd be craving this."

The class nodded wholeheartedly.

Mr. Bambuckle gently tossed the marshmallow across the campfire. It sailed through the tips of three—maybe four—flames before landing in Vinnie's hands.

"It's perfectly cooked!" she exclaimed, popping it into her mouth.

"A most wonderful roasting method, refined by generations of mountain women in Eastern Europe," said the teacher.

Albert shook his head in wonder. "You learn something new *twice* every day."

Snap!

"What was that?" said Evie, looking startled.

Somewhere in the dark, it sounded like a fallen twig had been broken in two.

Snap!

"There it is again," said Evie, chewing her fingernails.

Dodger fluttered down from the evening sky and landed on Mr. Bambuckle's shoulder, twittering a message.

The students sat frozen around the fire, their ears straining through the dark. Something was moving behind the cover of the trees.

Crack!

"The speckled-dagger vulture," whispered Albert.

"If there's one thing to say," said Mr. Bambuckle,

seemingly unaware of the tension, "it's that kindness is a most underrated possession."

Scarlett, who was feeling as anxious as Evie, frowned. "There's something lurking in the woods, and all you can think about is kindness?"

"Yes, kindness," said the teacher. "That and teamwork...and *barnacles*."

"Barnacles?" said Evie, her teeth chattering. "As in—"

Snap!

Mr. Bambuckle simply smiled. "Miss Frost, do kindly join us."

The students tensed up as Blue Valley School's assistant principal stepped into the light of the fire. She was dressed smartly in a white outfit and accompanied by a stylish camping bag, having no doubt come straight from her office at school. Her long, silver hair was brushed up into her trademark bun, and the diamond bobby pin that held it in place flickered in the orange light of the fire.

Despite her model looks, she put goose bumps on the arms of the children.

"How long have you been listening to us?" asked Ren.

Miss Frost raised a finger to remind Ren not to call out. "Long enough to know you are wasting precious learning time with ridiculous stories."

Vinnie's shoulders slumped. She had poured her heart and soul into sharing her tale.

Albert put his hand in the air.

"It had better be good," said Miss Frost. Her voice was an icy whisper.

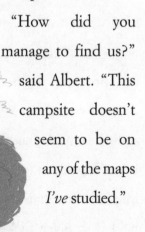

"How did you manage to find us?" said Albert. "This campsite doesn't seem to be on any of the maps *I've* studied."

Miss Frost's breath was misty against the evening sky. "Let's just say I've decided to embrace technology." She pulled out a small GPS monitor from her bag and rattled her car keys, adding, "I tracked you here—the bus. Your teacher's position at Blue Valley School is under constant review, and I'm here to ensure this camp meets all the required outcomes."

The callous teacher flicked a cold glance in Scarlett's direction. It was clear that she hadn't forgotten about the time she'd been zapped to Ecuador by a computer program.

The students' mouths fell open. It was one thing to have Miss Frost do a spot check at school but an entirely different thing to be ambushed at camp.

"We are always the better for your company," said Mr. Bambuckle cheerily.

Miss Frost dismissed the compliment with a flat reply. "You have broken occupational health and safety rule 756-H."

Mr. Bambuckle slapped his thigh and laughed. "I'd forget my head if it wasn't screwed on. I know the rule well."

"Then perhaps you'll tell me what the rule is." Miss Frost was playing it cool, and she was enjoying having power over the teacher.

"Rule 756-H states that no food may be thrown *over* a fire."

Miss Frost's lips twitched. She hadn't expected a correct response. "In any case, you broke the rule. I could have you fired for this."

Mr. Bambuckle laughed. "A most wonderful pun! I see what you did there…*fired*! Your jokes are really *hot*!"

Miss Frost was not impressed. She straightened her skirt and frowned at the teacher.

"You'll be the *flame* of my heart if you can *match* me," added Mr. Bambuckle.

Miss Frost's frown turned into a glare.

"Do play along," sang Mr. Bambuckle. "My puns will soon be *extinguished* without your *blazing* input."

The students were shaking violently, desperately trying to contain their laughter.

"Rule 756-H is a serious matter," said Miss Frost, her voice stopping any shakes in their tracks. "I will have to report this to Mr. Sternblast."

Mr. Bambuckle was anything but fazed by the threat. "If I had indeed broken the rule, then I agree, it would be a most serious matter."

"You threw food over a fire," said Miss Frost. "Case closed."

"Not *over* the fire," said Mr. Bambuckle. "*Through* the fire. I believe there is a distinct difference."

Miss Frost's lips quivered ever so slightly. She had been caught out on a technicality. "Well, there's still the matter of your poor preparation. Camp planning rule 229-A clearly states—"

"You'll find this trip has been most thoughtfully considered," said the teacher. "I spent weeks planning ahead."

"Then explain the lack of food," said Miss Frost. "I've checked the bus, and I couldn't find a thing. I shone my flashlight into your tent, and all I could see was fruit punch concentrate and chocolate cookies. What are you expecting the children to eat? Surely, you have more nutritious meals planned than roasted marshmallows?"

Mr. Bambuckle grinned from ear to ear. "The delightful Cafeteria Carol would be most disappointed in your lack of faith. I had a word with her earlier, and she will be providing wondrous supplies for us, delivered by another of my splendid contacts."

Miss Frost was not convinced. "Prove it," she whispered, and for a split second, the fire seemed to dim, casting dark shadows as far as the tent where Vex slept.

Mr. Bambuckle retrieved his phone from one of the many pockets in his jacket. "Technology *is* a wonderful thing. I'm thrilled you've decided to embrace it. I recorded the whole conversation with Carol." He pressed play. "You're most welcome to listen."

The students stared in wonder at their heroic teacher. He had warded off Miss Frost's attacks with merry diplomacy and uncanny organization.

"*Snap*," whispered Carrot Grigson, just loud enough for Sammy to hear.

"Lol," said Sammy.

Conversations with Cafeteria Carol

CAFETERIA CAROL

MR. BAMBUCKLE

What do you want?

Do you usually answer the phone so charmingly?

Yes. Especially when I'm working.

Are you in the cafeteria now?

Of course I am.

Outstanding, lovely Carol.

Tell me this isn't who I think it is?

That depends on who you think it is?

That blasted Bambuckle!

She shoots and scores! You are awfully clever, dear Carol.

Why did you phone me?

It seemed the right thing to do.

Talking to me is never the right thing to do.

In this case, it is. There is something that only you are skilled enough to do. Therefore, I needed to call.

Is it cafeteria related?

It most certainly is, though not in the family kind of way.

Huh?

I mean, do cafeterias have brothers or sisters?

What?

Or mothers or fathers?

You truly are a weird man.

Or third cousins once removed, for that matter?

What are you talking about?

Cafeterias don't have relatives. I am simply trying to clarify.

But what you want is cafeteria related?

Correct. Though not through blood.

There is no blood in the cafeteria!

That's not what the children say. They believe you store all sorts of horrors in there.

It's all lies! I hate the little critters.

Perhaps one day you'll come around and love them for who they are.

That's never going to happen.

You may surprise yourself yet.

Enough of this nonsense.
What do you want?

I would like enough food to feed fifteen children for three days.

Ha!

What's so funny?

Your joke.

It wasn't a joke, dear Carol.

You seriously want enough food for fifteen students for three days?

Of course not. How foolish of me.

Thought so.

I forgot to mention the two adults.

Two adults?

That's right. Enough food for fifteen children and two adults—for three days.

You have to be out of your mind. I can't cater for that many people with such short notice.

Ah, this is where your skills come into play.

What skills?

Your supplying skills.

Supplying skills?
Do you ever make sense?

If you could kindly *supply* enough food for fifteen students and two adults for three days, I'll have someone collect it. You don't need to *prepare* the food, simply *provide* it.

Oh. That seems doable.

You are a rare treasure, lovely Carol.

When do you need it by?

As soon as possible would be quite brilliant.

Say "please."

I most certainly will.

Do it.

Do what?

Say "please"!

Indeed.

Argh! Just say it for once!

It for once.

No, say that other word!

That other word.

Argh! Say the word starting with *P*.

Polyglot?

Huh? What on earth is a polyglot?

Someone who can speak multiple languages.

Why are you telling me this?

Because you asked.

I asked you to say "please."

That you did.

Look, I've got better things to be doing.

Such as?

Polishing my rolling pins.

A most honorable pastime.

What do you want? What food do you need?

There's a list near the phone.

Huh?

A list. Near the phone.

Where?

Beside your wrestling magazines.

Oh. How did that get there?

I have my methods.

That's just freaky.

Did you find the list?

I'm holding it now.

Splendid!

Okay. I'll do it. I'll supply the food
if it means you'll stop bothering me.

What would I do without you, Carol?

Starve to death.

We certainly couldn't have that.

It comes to $864.

A bargain basement buy. You'll find
the money is already in your account.

Impossible! Let me check... It's true!
How did you do it so quickly?

I know some people.

You are bizarre.

Your compliments make the sun shine brighter, dear Carol.

Who's going to pick up the food?

I believe it's already been picked up.

You seriously don't expect me to believe that.

Have a look and see for yourself. I ordered ten loaves of bread, two tubs of butter, eight heads of lettuce, two pounds of–

I know what the order is!
Let me take a look at the supplies...
I must be dreaming! They've all been taken!

Just as I expected. It should be arriving at camp as soon as this recording stops playing.

Recording? What recording?

The one Miss Frost is listening to now.

Huh?

You've been a fantastic help.

Can you do me a favor?

Anything.

Never, ever, ever call me again.

I think I can handle that.

Do you promise?

I most certainly do.

Really?

Yes, although I have one condition.

What's that?

Only if you say "please."

4

Kindness and Teamwork

Miss Frost tapped her foot impatiently. "And where exactly is the food you ordered?"

Mr. Bambuckle pointed to the twisted gum tree in the center of the campground. "Inside there, of course. Freshly delivered."

Miss Frost turned just in time to see the shadow of an incredibly short man vanish into the thick scrub.

"Tell that marvelous boss of yours I owe him one," called Mr. Bambuckle.

"He says he owes *you*," sang a friendly reply from somewhere in the dark.

Miss Frost's lips twitched at the irregularity of the

situation. Although she tried hard not to show it, she was furious with frustration. Mr. Bambuckle's methods were highly unorthodox, and she didn't like them one little bit.

She advanced toward the tree, examining the inside of its trunk with her flashlight. There were piles of provisions and fresh food, all of it packed safely in a variety of cooling bags and plastic containers. There was silverware and a toaster and everything in between—gas stoves, utensils, plates, and cups. The resourceful teacher had triumphed.

"We would be most honored if you'd join us for dinner," said Mr. Bambuckle. "I budgeted for fifteen children and *two* adults."

Miss Frost's reply was chilling. "Dinner is the last thing on my mind. I've come to assess you and your so-called strategies. I'll have you know I'm staying for the entire duration of camp, and I *will* catch you breaking rules. Discipline is the new order."

Scarlett, who was feeling a little vulnerable, fidgeted on her seat.

"How delightful," said Mr. Bambuckle. "If you're staying for the whole camp, then we shall enjoy your company all the more." He placed a log on the fire, quenching its thirst for fuel.

The evening stars were piercing the night sky. The children had never seen such a bright, starry display. Even Albert, who often enjoyed spending his evenings peering through a telescope, was impressed. "I should have brought my journal," he said. "The sky's a celebration of constellations!"

The students had had such fun setting up their tents and listening to Vinnie's story, they hadn't realized how hungry they'd become. The marshmallows, as tasty as they were, had simply roused their appetites.

"Now, who would like to help with dinner?" said Mr. Bambuckle, addressing the students.

"Yes, please!" chorused the class, all of them eager to please their teacher.

"Not so fast," said Miss Frost. "There are standards

that must be observed." She slid out a thick folder from her bag and opened it to the first page. "I expect you've followed these protocols." She sat down on one of the logs and tapped the space beside her, inviting Mr. Bambuckle into the frightening world of paperwork. "As for the students," she added, "I expect them to wait patiently."

Before adhering to Miss Frost's demands, Mr. Bambuckle turned to the children. "Kindness and teamwork—you'll know what to do."

☆ ☆ ☆

"Don't look at me," said Ren Rivera. "I may be good at detecting, but I've got no clue in this case. Miss Frost is not one for being interrupted."

"They've been poring over that folder for ages," said Sammy with a groan. "My stomach is rumbling louder than Slugger's snoring."

"Why are there so many rules Mr. Bambuckle has to follow?" complained Myra.

"Because Miss Frost is changing our school," said Victoria. "Remember, discipline is the new order."

"I can't take this much longer," said Sammy. "I'm so hungry, I could eat a hose."

"I think you mean *house*," said Slugger.

"I'm sure it's *hearse*," said Damon.

"I'm so hungry I could eat a harp," suggested Vinnie.

"Horse!" corrected Albert.

"Kindness and teamwork," pondered Miffy Armstrong, flexing the toned muscles in her arm. "Maybe we should get dinner ready ourselves? We could cook something yummy for the teachers."

"That's it!" cried Victoria. "How selfish of us not to figure it out. We've been too busy complaining about our empty tummies. We should be looking outward, not inward."

Damon was the first to agree with Victoria. "What *she* said!"

"Absolutely brilliant!" said Harold. "Let's make dinner."

"We'll need a head chef," said Miffy.

"Slugger!" The decision was unanimous.

Miss Frost, while usually one to take pleasure in catching children breaking rules, was so committed to torturing Mr. Bambuckle with checklists and regulations that she failed to notice the students moving about. Mr. Bambuckle, on the other hand, kept one eye on the protocols and the other on his class. His chest filled with pride as they stealthily set to work.

Miffy and Sammy used their strength to unpack and carry a card table over from the bus.

"I'm stronger than a fox," said Sammy.

"I think you mean *stronger than a box*," said Miffy.

"Ox!" called Albert from the other side of the campsite.

They set up the table beneath the twisted gum tree before tending to the fire, which required another log. Even the sudden burst of flames wasn't enough to draw Miss Frost's gray-blue eyes away from her folder.

Harold and Myra passed things from the hollow trunk to Slugger as he asked for them. The table soon became the sturdy base of a makeshift kitchen.

Slugger, who had enlisted the help of Scarlett and Carrot, instructed his sous chefs to prepare the vegetables for the main course. Scarlett peeled the potatoes while Carrot peeled the carrots, something he had always loved doing.

Fresh water was carted from the nearby river in small containers by Albert and Victoria. They made multiple trips by flashlight, never complaining, and boiled the water over the fire before pouring it into a large plastic tub that acted as a sink.

Damon, who was jealous of the time Albert got

to spend with Victoria, pushed the thoughts away for the greater good. He took the next best possible job that interested him—rinsing the snow peas and beans in the sink. He beamed every time Victoria returned from the river with more water.

Evie was Damon's assistant, enjoying the fact she could wash and rinse without being attacked by an appliance. She had once had a nasty experience with a washing machine, but it seemed like a distant memory now.

Ren and Vinnie, as only best friends can, brainstormed dessert ideas. Slugger was feeling generous and had asked for a suggestion.

"Chocolate mousse?" said Ren.

"We don't have any cream," said Vinnie. "What about Popsicles?"

"No freezer," said Ren.

"Jell-O?"

"Too wobbly."

"Pancakes?"

"Mr. Bambuckle's specialty."

While they couldn't agree to begin with, the best friends' telepathy was in scrumptious synchronization as they both thought back to their first sleepover. "Chocolate-dipped Rice Krispies Treats!" they cried together.

"Chocolate-dipped Rice Krispies Treats it is," said Slugger.

Mr. Bambuckle shook his head in amazement. The class was tapping into their true potential, and he felt honored to be witnessing it.

"Why are you shaking your head?" hissed Miss Frost. "Do you not understand the importance of section 36-P?"

"Indeed, I understand," said the teacher. He turned back to the folder but not before glancing over his shoulder into the trees.

Peter Strayer was absent from the bulk of the action in the clearing. He was busy roaming deep in the woods, setting up something special at Mr. Bambuckle's request. Earlier, he had discovered a note in his bag explaining what he had to do. Right now, he was jumping between fallen logs and mossy ground, the teacher's note and his flashlight his only guides.

The one student not buzzing with productivity was Vex. He remained fast asleep in his tent, unaware of all the positive energy outside.

As Slugger finished plating the main course, the rest of the students banded together to set up a picnic area. They spread blankets over the grass in the clearing and laid them with silverware and drinking cups. Using dozens of tea lights, they lit the area so it sparkled with the soft glow of quality dining. It was truly a masterpiece in design.

If the students were pleased with their picnic setup, it was nothing compared to how they would feel about Slugger's cuisine. The bulky chef had dished up fire-cooked chicken with honeyed carrots, buttered potatoes, and lemon greens. On a large tray, he had prepared Belgian-chocolate-dipped Rice Krispies Treats and garnished them with flakes of toffee. The smell was divine.

"There's more water in my mouth than in the river," said Sammy. "Let's eat!"

"Wait," said Victoria. "We need to make sure every-thing is perfect. Our teachers deserve the best, even if one of them can be a little cruel at times."

"A little?" said Scarlett, who hadn't forgotten the way Miss Frost looked at her when she first arrived at camp.

"At times?" said Harold.

Victoria insisted. "We've put in so much effort already. Finishing strong is just as important."

"Agreed," said Damon.

The children moved to the picnic area, taking with them the steaming plates of chicken as well as the dessert tray. Slugger quickly added slices of lime to six jugs of water and had Scarlett and Carrot place them in the center of each blanket. Everything was in place. Everything was perfect.

"You invite the teachers over," whispered Victoria, nudging Miffy. "It was your idea."

"Kindness and teamwork," whispered Miffy, and she cleared her throat. "Excuse me, Mr. Bambuckle and Miss Frost, we've made dinner for you."

The children straightened up, standing shoulder to shoulder, the proof of their hard work on display in their hands. They were framed by the tea lights, and the wide smiles on their faces paraded their pride.

Only Mr. Bambuckle looked up at the happy class, his breath immediately taken away. "Oh my."

Miss Frost simply snapped the folder shut and turned toward the bus. "I'd rather eat my own food. I'll be staying in my car if anyone needs me."

With a sniff, she walked away without even acknowledging the students' efforts.

The children were hurt. The cold reality of Miss Frost's character stung like an icicle to the heart. Mr. Bambuckle knew this, and his enthusiasm soon restored their spirits. "This is the most astonishing dinner I have *ever* had the privilege of smelling."

Slugger mustered a smile. "Thank you," he said. "Just wait until you taste it."

"Indeed," said Mr. Bambuckle. With that, he motioned to the blankets, knocking Carrot's plate out of his hand. It clattered onto the ground. "How very careless of me, dear Carrot. I'm sincerely sorry."

Carrot's jaw dropped. He had never known his teacher to be clumsy. "I was looking forward to eating that."

Sammy, who had been drooling impatiently, delved deep into his conscience. "You can share with me, Carrot."

"That's very kind of you, Sammy," said Mr.

Bambuckle, "but as Miss Frost won't be joining us, her plate has Carrot's name on it. Now, let's eat!"

The teacher, surrounded by his beloved class, sat among the tea lights and feasted on what was a truly delicious dinner. They ate and laughed and sipped lime water until their bellies ached. They recalled humorous moments from the afternoon until satisfied yawns filled the air.

"We have a big day tomorrow," said the teacher. "Miss Frost has a rather wonderful challenge planned."

"Fantastic," said Miffy, groaning. "Just what we need—a challenge from Miss Frost. *That* can't be good."

"It *will* be difficult," admitted Mr. Bambuckle, "but of your success, I am most certain."

The students cleared away their plates and stacked them in the washing tub.

"I'll clean them," volunteered Vinnie, "and I'm not just doing it to suck up."

"A most thoughtful gesture," said Mr. Bambuckle.

The rest of the class waved their thanks to Vinnie before disappearing one by one into their tents. Ren, as best friends do, stayed back to help wash up.

Damon, the only tent-less student, shuffled happily around his sleeping bag. "*I* get to enjoy the open sky."

"Good night, Damon," said the teacher. "Sleep tight."

The Subtle Art of Catching Zs
Damon Dunst's Story

Thousands of stars are winking at me. They look like silver pinpricks in the clear night sky. Maybe forgetting a tent was a good thing after all. It beats staring up at a boring canvas roof.

The sleeping bag is nice and warm. Mr. Bambuckle was very kind to lend it to me. My toes wriggle around, searching for fresh pockets of snugness.

Ah, this is the life. The open sky. Victoria in a tent nearby. Hey, that rhymes. I'll have to remember to add it to my book of romantic song lyrics. I can hear the melody now… *The open sky, Victoria in a tent nearby.* She'll love this song. When it's ready, I'll use it to win her heart.

Not that I've actually finished writing a song before. Uncle Rick always teases me about my songwriting. "You'll never finish a song, Damon," he says. "You get too distracted. You haven't got what it takes. Songwriting is a lot harder than you realize."

It's all right for him. His tunes have won awards and been played on the radio. He could be a little more encouraging though. He knows it's a goal of mine to finally complete a song.

The open sky, Victoria in a tent nearby… She stares into my eyes…

Hmmm, how would she be staring into my eyes if she's in her tent? Maybe her tent has a hole in it…

The open sky, Victoria in a tent nearby. She cuts a hole in her tent…

But I suppose it's dark at night. She wouldn't be able

to see anything anyway. Even if her tent had a hole and she was looking in my general direction, the darkness would cover my good looks. She'd need a light…

The open sky, Victoria in a tent nearby. She cuts a hole in her tent, turns on the flashlight she rents.

Rental flashlights. What will they think of next? Yeah, I'll add that to my lyric book tomorrow. Perfect. Maybe I'll even finish the song. Maybe I won't get distracted by other thoughts.

I suppose I'd better get some sleep. Mr. Bambuckle said we have a big day tomorrow. I wonder what Miss Frost has planned? No doubt she'll try to make life miserable. It's a good thing we have Mr. Bambuckle on our side.

Sleep.

I close my eyes, but there's a blob of light on my eyelids where the moon was. Hee-hee. It looks funny.

But seriously, I had better get some rest.

Ah…

The open sky, Victoria in a tent nearby…

Hang on. What's that? I think I can hear snoring.

Yep. Definitely snoring.

I sit up. Who is it?

Hmmm...it seems to be coming from Slugger's direction. I can just make out the silhouette of his tent in the moonlight.

Must sleep.

Okay. This is annoying now. His snoring is getting louder. It sounds like somebody is rubbing a giant, slobbery oyster over a bed of gravel. Gross, moist crunchiness. Now I'm picturing what that would look like. Disturbing. Do giant oysters even exist?

Stop snoring, Slugger. It's not good for your androids. Or is it adenoids? Albert would know.

Slugger is getting louder. Maybe I should go and roll him over.

Dang. A cloud just covered the moon. Thankfully, there's enough starlight.

I tiptoe over to his tent.

Zzziiippp.

Why are tent zippers so loud when you undo them slowly?

I wedge my hands under Slugger's right shoulder. He's very heavy. It takes all my strength, but I manage to roll him onto his side. He mumbles something about too much pepper. And he's stopped snoring.

ZIP!

Oops. Maybe slower zipping is the quietest method after all.

Slugger is awake. "Who's there? What are you doing?"

"Sorry, Slugger. You were snoring, so I rolled you over. I couldn't sleep."

"Go back to bed, Damon."

"I will. Sorry."

I steal back to my sleeping bag and wriggle into a comfortable position. I feel a little guilty for waking Slugger. I suppose it's better than total eardrum torture.

Ah…

The open sky, Victoria in a tent nearby. She cuts a hole in her tent…

This is the life. I have just penned the beginning of what could be my first complete song, and now it's time for some quality rest.

Oh no. Not again. Slugger has drifted off, and now he's snoring even louder.

Maybe I should try counting sheep.

☆ ☆ ☆

One, two, three, four… Hee-hee, that sheep has green wool. Isn't there a book about a green sheep?

Focus, Damon.

One, two, three, four, five, six…

I wonder what Victoria is dreaming about right now? I hope it's me.

Come on, focus!

One, two, three, four, five, six, seven, eight, nine…

There are an awful lot of sheep in this pen. Have I imagined enough room to keep them hemmed in?

Dang! There's a hole in the fence, and the sheep are escaping! Nine, eight, seven, six, five, four—there goes the green sheep—three, two, one.

No sheep left.

The farmer is going to kill me. His sheep have broken out, *plus* there's a hole in his fence.

He's coming over, and he's not happy. He's yelling at me for losing the sheep. He says I have to round them

up and fix his fence. I run away because I'm scared. I run straight into the arms of Victoria.

Ah…that's a nicer thought. I feel much better when I'm around Victoria. She puts spiders in my tummy. Or maybe not spiders—they'd be all bitey and scratchy. More like ice-cream soda foam—she makes my tummy fizzy and bubbly.

Victoria is smiling, and she asks me to try counting sheep again. Okay, Victoria, I'll do it for you.

I imagine a much kinder farmer. He's offered to *pay* me to count sheep. Anything for you, sir.

One, two, three, four—hello, green sheep—five, six, seven, eight, nine, ten, eleven, twelve, thirteen… Huh? There aren't any sheep left. I have literally run out of sheep to count.

I tell the nice farmer. He can only smile in reply. He's not even angry. I inform him that friendliness doesn't compensate for lack of investment sensibility. With more sheep, his profit margins will increase. There would also be enough sheep to help people like me get to sleep.

The kind farmer doesn't know what to do. He shrugs his shoulders and walks away.

Wait, come back!

My stomach gives a little rumble. All this thinking about sheep has made me hungry.

I could down a juicy lamb chop. Maybe I'll count those instead. One lamb chop, two lamb chops, three lamb chops, four lamb chops... Gross! That chop is green! Is it moldy? I don't want to get food poisoning. Then I'd *never* fall asleep!

This is ridiculous. Counting sheep was the worst idea ever. I have to think of something else.

I once heard someone say that cooling off can help you sleep. I think I'll try that.

☆ ☆ ☆

I take off my shirt and shove it in my bag. I feel cooler already.

Ah...

The open sky, Victoria in a tent nearby. She cuts a hole in her tent…

I'll have to try to finish the song tomorrow. Uncle Rick says the best tunes are written in moments of inspiration. He may poke fun at me about never finishing my songs, but I have a good feeling about this one. I think I'll find that magical moment of inspiration.

This is so much better. Why didn't I think of cooling down earlier?

The open sky, Victoria in a tent nearby. She cuts a hole in her tent…

The melody is strong in my head. Victoria is going to love it once I'm done.

I wonder what time it is. The stars have been inching across the sky.

Bzzzzz… Bzzzzz… Bzzz… Bzzzzz…

What's that?

Bzzzzz… Bzzzzz… Bzzzzz…

It's a mosquito!

Slap!

Missed.

Bzzzzz…

It's landed on my face.

Slap!

Ouch!

Missed.

Bzzzzz…

I flap my arms around like one of those wacky inflatable car lot men. I've never understood that. Come and buy our cars. We'll lure you in with the old tall-blow-up-person-having-a-heart-attack technique. Strange. Though I suppose it keeps the mosquitoes away. There's nothing worse than making an important financial decision while you're itchy.

Bzzzzz… Bzzzzz… Bzzzzz…

Okay, I've got you now, mosquito.

Slap!

Gotcha!

Yuk.

I can feel a tiny patch of gooiness on my palm. It has the sloppy consistency of insect guts mixed with human blood. Disgusting. I rub it onto my shorts. That's better.

Finally, peace and quiet. No snoring. No insects. Just me and the midnight sky, the cool air on my bare chest.

Bzzzzz... Bzzz... Bzzzz... Bzzzz... Bzzzzz...

Bzzzzz... Bzzz... Bzzzzz...

Bzzzzz... Bzzz... Bzzzz... Bzzzz... Bzzzzz...

Bzzzzz... Bzzz... Bzzzzz...

Bzzzzz... Bzzz... Bzzzz... Bzzzz... Bzzzzz...

Argh! Hundreds of mosquitoes descend upon my exposed skin. They're out for revenge. I murdered their friend, and now they're taking their pound of flesh. And blood. Why couldn't they have gone to the squashed mosquito's funeral and left me alone?

Bzzzzz... Bzzz... Bzzzzz...

Bzzzzz... Bzzz... Bzzzz... Bzzzz... Bzzzzz...

Bzzzzz… Bzzz… Bzzzz… Bzzzz… Bzzzzz…

Bzzzzz… Bzzz… Bzzzzz…

I stand up and flail my arms wildly. I have become the inflatable car lot man. I wave so hard, my feet almost lift off the ground. I swat and swipe and slap and strike. My arms almost come out of their sockets.

Bzzzzz… Bzzzzz…

I rummage through my bag.

Bzzzzz… Bzzzzz…

I throw on my shirt.

Bzzzzz… Bzzzzz…

I find a can of insect repellent.

Ssshhh!

Enough spray to last a lifetime.

Silence.

The mosquitoes have retreated to their hiding places.

I climb back into the sleeping bag and try not to scratch my itchy chest. I should have stayed in the sleeping bag all along. Rookie error.

Must sleep. Getting tired.

My mom once told me that imagining your favorite place helps you fall asleep. I think I'll try that.

I imagine knocking on the front door of Victoria's house. This is *definitely* my favorite place.

Mr. Goldenhorn opens the door. "Damon, we've been expecting you. Victoria hasn't stopped telling us how much she's been looking forward to your visit."

I like this method of falling asleep.

Mr. Goldenhorn points me in the direction of the living room. "She'll be so excited to see you."

Victoria is sitting on the couch. She is wearing a frilly blue dress, and her long, blond hair shimmers against it. Her lips are glowing with strawberry lip gloss. She is a picture of heaven.

She leaps up when she sees me and rushes over, throwing her arms around my neck. "I've missed you, Damon darling!" She takes my hand, and we sit down together.

The lights dim, and romantic music plays from the speakers near the television. Victoria squeezes my hand and whispers in my ear, "You're my charming teddy bear."

Goose bumps.

I'm about to tell her I love her when I notice something strange. "Your hair smells like a farmyard."

Victoria raises an eyebrow as if to tell me I'm imagining things—which I suppose technically I am—then she leans close to kiss me. She slowly pouts her lips, and I shut my eyes in readiness.

Baa-aa.

I open my eyes to find I'm staring straight into the face of a sheep. It's wearing a frilly blue dress, and its glossy lips are pressed together. It's leaning in for a kiss.

"Argh!" I leap off the couch. "Victoria, what happened to you?"

Baa-aa. The frilly-blue-dress sheep bounds after me, gunning for the kiss. It charges at me, but I sidestep at the last moment, catching a whiff of its grassy breath. That was close.

I dash up the hallway toward the backyard. The sheep trots after me. It's clip-clopping after my heart.

I stumble into the bright sunlight of the back garden.
A horrible sight greets me.

Baa-aa-aa… Baa… Baa-aa-aa… Baa-aa-aa-aa… Baa…

Baa… Baa-aa-aa… Baa-aa… Baa…

Baa-aa… Baa-aa… Baa-aa-aa-aa… Baa-aa-aa…

Baa-aa-aa… Baa… Baa-aa-aa… Baa-aa-aa-aa… Baa…

Baa… Baa-aa-aa… Baa-aa… Baa…

Hundreds of sheep have formed a semicircle around
me. One of them is green—the fourth in the line if I count
correctly. They press in on me. The frilly-blue-dress sheep
is smacking its strawberry lips in my direction.

Bzzzzz…

The sheep suddenly morph into maddened
mosquitoes. Their suckers pulsate in bloodthirsty
hunger. Or is it blood-hungry thirst? They buzz their
wings angrily in anti-repellent protest. The biggest
mosquito—dressed in a frilly blue dress—has lip gloss
smeared over its razor-sharp sucker. It aims for my neck
and darts forward.

A sleepwalking, snoring Slugger appears from nowhere and bashes the frilly-blue-dress mosquito with a closed fist. The mosquito reels backward and explodes into fine, blue powder. This scares the rest of the swarm, and they buzz off faster than I can say "buzz off."

Slugger and I stand alone in the backyard. "Thanks," I say.

But Slugger can't hear me. He's still asleep, and his snoring has reached insanity levels. It sounds like whoever was rubbing the giant oyster over a bed of gravel has amplified the hideous noise through the world's loudest loudspeaker.

I will never fall asleep like this. *Never.*

I need a new strategy, or the night will be gone. The subtle art of catching Zs is proving harder than I thought.

☆ ☆ ☆

I stare at the moon and stars. The sky around them has changed from black to gray. My eyelids are heavy, but my thoughts are like helium-filled balloons. I can't keep them down. There has to be *something* I can do to fall asleep before the sun comes up.

Music. Of course. Mom and Dad used to play music to help me sleep when I was a baby. I have hundreds of songs on my phone, but Mom made me leave it at home.

I wonder if Slugger brought *his* phone?

I creep across to his tent.

Zzziiippp.

The fading moonlight reveals his bag is near his head. I'll have to be stealthy. I inch closer and lift the bag away. Slugger stirs and mumbles something about finishing a job. He enjoys a good mutter in his sleep.

The bag is closed.

Zzziiippp.

My fingers wriggle in exploration. I grasp something small and solid. It feels rectangular. I pull it out and squint through the dull light. It's a phone!

It's not password protected, and I'm able to swipe open the home screen. Soft, blue light reflects on my face.

I touch the music icon but can't believe my eyes. There's not a single song on Slugger's phone.

There's a podcast icon, and I press it in hope. There are plenty of downloads here, so I scroll through them.

There is no music. Dejected, I put the phone back into Slugger's bag and close it.

Zzziiippp.

I step out of his tent.

Zzziiippp.

Sleep shouldn't be this difficult. I sneak back to my camping area and sit down. The gray sky is becoming lighter by the minute. I know music will help me catch some Zs, but where to find it?

I suppose I could make my own music. I could try singing to myself. Maybe I could try to finish the song for Victoria without getting distracted. I could prove to Uncle Rick that I have it in me to complete a full composition after all.

I remember the melody, but before I belt out the first note, I stop. Something is missing. The song needs an accompaniment, a musical instrument of some sort.

Drums!

That's what the song needs.

There are some enormous pots and pans on the card table. They'd make awesome drums. I can see their dark outlines against the twisted tree.

I'll need something to hit them with. Maybe some of the leftover marshmallow sticks...

The sun breaks the horizon with a gentle golden glow. I grip my drumsticks and ready myself for the song. If everything goes according to plan, I'll be sound asleep in a few minutes. I take a deep breath and pause. It's the first sunrise I have ever seen, and it's more beautiful than I could have imagined. A wave of inspiration gushes over me. Distraction free, my thoughts crystallize.

BOOM!

"The open sky..."

BOOM, BOOM!

"Victoria in a tent nearby..."

CRASH, BOOM, CRASH!

"She cuts a hole in her tent…"

BOOM, BOOM, BOOM!

"Turns on the flashlight she rents…"

CRASH, CRASH, BOOM!

"She shines the light at my eyes…"

BOOM, BA-DUM BOOM, BOOM!

"I can't see. Am I going blind?"

CRASH! CRASH!

"I'm blindly in love."

BOOM, BOOM, BOOM, BOOM!

I did it! I actually finished a song. I managed to complete an entire tune without becoming distracted. Uncle Rick was wrong. I *have* got what it takes!

Mr. Bambuckle's tent zips open, and he steps outside. The early morning sun shines on his face. "That, dear Damon, was the most wonderful way to start the day. I'll be sure to let my rock star cousin in Iceland know about your tune." He blinks brightly at my improvised drum kit. "And a splendid way to…*snare* a girl's heart, I might add."

I can hear the contented sighs of my classmates as they begin to emerge from their tents.

"Best sleep I've had in months," says Scarlett.

"I slept like a baby," says Harold.

"I slept like a log," says Albert.

"I slept *on* a log," says Carrot. "It was surprisingly comfortable."

I can only shake my head in jealous disbelief. Even Miss Frost, who has returned from sleeping in her car, is looking fresh. Her silver hair and diamond bobby pin glisten in the morning light.

Victoria is the last to surface. "Good morning, everyone. What a gorgeous sunrise." She plucks a piece of blue wool from her pajamas before spotting me and the pots and pans. "Oh, did I miss something?"

5

The Challenge

Without the distraction of hammering Mr. Bambuckle with rules and guidelines from her folder, Miss Frost's focus was well and truly on the children that morning.

"You shall not sit any closer than two yards from the fire."

"Brush your teeth again. Bacon and eggs are a nasty combination, and the taste should be scrubbed away."

"Tidy your tents or face my wrath."

"Wear two pairs of socks, since you'll be doing a lot of running today."

"Go to the bathroom before we start. Not on the

side of a tree, Hairball McDarryl. This isn't the Scottish Highlands. Detention back at school!"

The students looked to Mr. Bambuckle for help. His attention, however, was with Dodger. He was whispering mischievously to the blue jay, who fluttered excitedly on his shoulder.

Miss Frost signaled for the students to gather on the logs around the smoldering fire. "A minimum of two yards," she reminded them. "And where are Rex and Dieter?"

"They'll be sitting this activity out," explained Mr. Bambuckle, who had a knack for knowing when to intervene. His voice carried well-timed authority, and the assistant principal didn't press further. Peter was free to be absent, and Vex was free to continue resting.

Miss Frost's icy stare subdued the students into complete silence. "I have a *challenge* for you, one that will cover a number of outdoor education outcomes as well as test your orientation skills."

Mr. Bambuckle rubbed his hands together in anticipation.

"I have not forgotten the abhorrent crime one of you inflicted on me when I taught in room 12B," continued Miss Frost. She looked directly at Scarlett. "You there, stand up."

"Me?" said Scarlett.

"Who else do you think I'm speaking to?"

Scarlett rose, biting her bottom lip.

"I am not so easily fooled," said Miss Frost. "I know it was *you* who schemed to get rid of me, Starlett. I know it was *you* who caused all sorts of strange things to happen when *you* were on the computer. I know it was *you* who zapped me to Ecuador."

Scarlett could only tremble in reply. Everything the assistant principal said was true. She *had* used a computer program—PhotoCrop—to transport Miss Frost to South America.

"Do you deny it?" said Miss Frost.

Scarlett glanced at Mr. Bambuckle, and even though

she only brushed his gaze, there was something about the sparkle in his green eyes that told her to take heart. "It's true," she said boldly.

The rest of the students wriggled uncomfortably, terrified of the outcome of this admission.

"That wasn't so hard, was it?" hissed Miss Frost. "And now, I have you right where I want you."

Mr. Bambuckle winked at Scarlett, who was looking pale at the unfolding nightmare.

"Back to the task at hand," said Miss Frost, now addressing everyone. "It would appear your classmate is in deep trouble. There will be severe consequences for her actions."

Scarlett's face drained of all color.

"But since I too can enjoy a good game," said Miss Frost, "I'm giving you a chance to save your classmate. If Starlett is to be spared from punishment, one of you must defeat me in a challenge."

Mr. Bambuckle could barely contain his grin. He

fidgeted with the excitement of a schoolboy before his first soccer match.

Myra raised her hand.

"Yes, Miley?"

"It's Myra. What exactly is the challenge?"

Miss Frost's diamond bobby pin flashed coldly. "The challenge is plain and simple, and it involves a touch of technology—something I am beginning to grow quite fond of. How ironic that Charlotte's fate will depend on technology."

"But what do we have to do?" pressed Myra.

"I will give each of you a tracking band to wear on your wrist. You'll then have a ten-minute head start to run off into the woods. After that time, I will come searching for you, tracking your signals. Consider it a giant game of hide and seek, with an element of tag. If I find you and catch you, you're out."

"That's not fair," said Sammy. "All you have to do is follow the GPS signals."

A wicked grin spread across Miss Frost's face. "Then you will need to keep moving at a rapid pace."

Sammy crossed his arms.

"If I track all of you down before noon," continued Miss Frost, "Scarborough will be disciplined severely. However, if I fail to catch just one of you, she will be spared. You must stay within the borders of the broader campsite—no crossing the river or any roads. Those are your boundaries."

Mr. Bambuckle was now bursting at the seams. "The best part is," he said, "Miss Frost was a state champion in athletics at high school. She even captained the national team!"

Miss Frost's jaw dropped. "How could you possibly know that?"

"I know everything," said Mr. Bambuckle.

"How is that a good thing?" said Sammy. "She'll win easily!"

The blue suit of the teacher dazzled the way it did

before something unusual happened. "It's a good thing," he replied, "because it will make your victory even sweeter."

Miss Frost dismissed the possibility of Mr. Bambuckle's remark with a smirk. "We'll see about that."

Two students, meanwhile, sat tapping small sticks on the logs they sat on. Albert and Myra had entered into a private conversation.

DOTS AND DASHES PASSED BETWEEN

ALBERT SMITHERS

AND

MYRA KUMAR

Do you know Morse code?

Is the Sahara hot?

Huh?

Do birds fly?

I'm not sure what you mean.

Is Miss Frost cruel?

What's with the questions?

They are rhetorical questions pertaining to the
fact that of course I know Morse code.

Couldn't you have just said yes?

Yes.

So you know Morse code?

Do I need to ask another rhetorical question?

Was that a rhetorical question?

Did it sound like a rhetorical question?

              I am so confused.

Don't be. I know Morse code.

              Finally, a straight answer.

Didn't you just assume from my answers that I know
Morse code?

              Was that yet another rhetorical
              question?

Not this time.

              Thank goodness.

Indeed.

              I have a money question.

Numbers are one of my *specialties*.

              I'm thinking about starting a
              business.

How exciting!

              Totally.

May I ask what the business is?

              It's top secret at this stage.

Fair enough.

              I need to know how much money is
              required to get it off the ground.

That's a difficult one to calculate without knowing
much about your business plan.

Let's just say it involves making a lot of cash-ola.

That doesn't really help me. Have you thought about asking your parents for help with the funds?

They told me to ask you. They said you'd be able to do the calculations faster than, and at the fraction of the cost of, a professional bank loaner.

I'm intrigued now. What fraction of the cost are we talking?

Zero zeroths to be precise.

I see.

Yep, a big fat nix.

Aha.

Nothing.

I understand.

Zilch.

I'm following.

Zip.

Yep.

Nada.

I get it.

I've run out of synonyms.

I figured you would at some point.

> Speaking of zero, it's quite profitable asking people to work for you for free.

I bet it is.

> That's part of my business model.

Free labor?

> Absolutely. The profit margins are off the hook.

I was chatting to Damon about profit margins.

> What did he have to say? Maybe I should ask him.

He said that farmers should buy lots and lots of sheep. He said something about it helping people fall asleep. Beats me what he was talking about.

> How odd.

Yes, I suspect poor Damon had taken a bump to the head.

> Hee-hee.

How did you come to learn Morse code, if you don't mind me asking?

> With the help of an app I found on the internet. It translates everything for me.

A genius idea.

How did you learn Morse?

I learned it from a book when I was two.

Why doesn't that surprise me?

Nice use of a rhetorical question.

Thanks.

When do you plan on launching the business?

Once we get back from camp.

You don't mess around.

Not when there's money to be made.

Good point.

I have a joke for you.

I like jokes.

When does it rain money?

Beats me.

When there is change in the weather.

I see what you did there.

Want to hear another?

Sure.

What did the cat say when he lost all his money?

I don't know.

I'm paw.

The first one was better.

What did the first accountant say to the second accountant?

I like the sound of this joke. What did the first accountant say to the second accountant?

Pass the stapler.

I don't get it.

He needed to staple some pieces of paper together.

But it's not funny.

No, it's very serious. The paper was for an important client's tax return.

I thought it was a joke.

Of course not. It was a busy day, and he had a massive pile of paperwork to sort through.

I suppose so.

Without staples, the pieces of paper could have been separated or blown away.

Is it usually windy in tax offices?

Huh?

I doubt the paper would have blown away.

They had the windows open.

You seem to know an awful lot about this tax office.

It's where I go to get advice from time to time.

I think you should go there to get advice for your business.

Now that I think about it, you're right.

Sorry I couldn't help with your number crunching.

That's okay.

Good luck with it all.

Thanks. Oh, Miss Frost wants us to line up for the challenge now.

I don't like the sound of the game she has planned.

Scarlett must be stressed out of her brain.

I know. Poor Scarlett.

Come on. Let's line up before we get in trouble.

Hide and Sneak

Miffy Armstrong's Story

I clip the GPS band around my wrist. I can feel the frantic beat of my pulse beneath the smooth plastic. I want to take it off, but Miss Frost would kill me.

The band reads 9:00. There are three hours until noon.

I join my classmates at the starting line. When the signal sounds, we'll have ten minutes to escape into the woods. Then we'll be tracked down like wild animals. It's terrifying, but it's our only chance to save Scarlett.

Poor Scarlett. Punishments shouldn't be decided by cruel games. The worst part is that Miss Frost seems to be taking some kind of sick pleasure out of the situation.

She stalks back and forth behind the line. Her last whisper puts goose bumps on the back of my neck. "When I find you—and I *will* find you—you must return immediately to the main campsite."

Mr. Bambuckle applauds from his seat under the twisted gum. "What fun!"

Miss Frost walks around in front of us. She has swapped her teaching outfit for an equally stylish white tracksuit. Her muscles are surprisingly toned. She looks like one of the senior athletes Coach Wyatt is always pointing out to me at workouts. "That could be you if you work hard enough," he says.

It certainly seems like Miss Frost has been training hard.

It could just be me, but I notice a dreamy expression

on Mr. Bambuckle's face every time he looks at her. It reminds me of the way Damon looks at Victoria.

Miss Frost blows a whistle. That's our signal.

We take off into the woods, tearing through the undergrowth as fast as we can. Before a minute is up, we've separated into different groups.

I can hear Evie sniffing back tears as she tries to keep up with me and Sammy at the front of the pack. I want to go back and help her, but it's best if we split up.

Myra is back to the left. I can hear her crashing over sticks and bushes and making as much noise as Damon's early morning serenade.

I grit my teeth and up the pace, thoughts of Scarlett driving me on. I pray Miss Frost doesn't come after me first. Sammy swerves off to the right. Maybe she'll go for him. Then again, maybe she'll target me because I'm the fastest.

After a few more minutes, I'm on my own. I stop and listen. I can hear distant rustles as my classmates scamper away in different directions. I can't see anyone, so I sit down and gather my breath.

Something yellow grabs my attention. A flower. It's sitting on top of a pointy rock a couple of yards away. The odd thing is, it's not attached to a stem. Someone must have placed it there. I crawl over—being sure to keep low to the ground—and pick it up. It's fresh.

I spot an identical flower wedged between two thin branches in a small tree. I creep over and pluck it out. Then I slip the flowers around my headband. They're pretty.

There's a third yellow flower on the ground just beyond the small tree. I get down

again and move over to pick it up. The chain of yellow is broken by something blue. A feather sparkles at the base of a much larger tree. I shuffle over and examine it, resting my back against the broad trunk of the gum. The blue plume glints and glistens, so I add it to my headband along with the third flower.

"No!" A shout cuts through the silence. It's Myra. Her voice is tight with fear. Worse than that, she's nearby. Too close for comfort.

I peer out from behind the tree and freeze. Myra is only a bus length away from where I'm sitting, and she's cornered by Miss Frost. The teacher reaches out a hand and tags her on the shoulder.

Myra looks devastated. She takes off her GPS band and hands it to Miss Frost, who slips it into her pocket and points in the direction of camp. Myra's shoulders slump forward as she trudges away.

Miss Frost stays still. She studies her GPS tracker and surveys the area. She must know I'm close. I pull back behind the tree and hold my breath.

Footsteps.

Slow and steady. Getting closer. So this is what it feels like to be hunted.

I dare not move a muscle. She's on the other side of the tree. I've been caught far too early, and I'm furious at myself for stopping to rest. Coach Wyatt would kill me for doing something like this. He's always telling me to push myself to new limits. "Rest comes after exhaustion," he says.

The footsteps suddenly take off. I turn to see Miss Frost running swiftly toward the river. She's spied Victoria and Harold, who are huddled behind a tall rock. They should have split up.

I exhale slowly. But I can't understand why she didn't catch me when I was so close. I check to make sure the band is working. Its tiny lights flash across the screen.

Perhaps Miss Frost wanted two for the price of one. In either case, I stand up and dash away before I can be seen.

☆ ☆ ☆

I slow to a trot, eyes peeled. I've been running for a few minutes now and should have put some distance between myself and Miss Frost.

Scarlett deserves better than this. She doesn't need the stress of this stupid game. Nobody does. Miss Frost was so hard on her back there, pressuring her into admitting what she did. It's not fair.

I ease to a stop and check out my surroundings. Nothing but trees. I've lost sight of the river and haven't come across any roads. I sit for another quick rest.

Coach Wyatt would be after me for taking a break. He'd be urging me on, telling me to elevate my game. Telling me I'll never make the state team if I don't have a mind and body of steel.

The state team.

My dream.

From the moment I started training with Coach Wyatt, I've had one goal: to make the state team. It's harder than it sounds. Everyone at school expects me to get there, but they haven't met the other athletes in my group. I'm not sure I'll ever be good enough. Especially when I suck at hurdles.

Hurdles.

My dream crusher.

Hurdles are literally the barrier blocking me from moving to the next level in my career. That's what Coach Wyatt calls it—my career. "You must train harder if you want to advance your career," he says. "The hurdles are stopping you from moving forward. It's all about your front leg. You need to raise it higher."

Apparently, he can't do much more with me until he sees improved hurdling. I don't know if I'll ever get there, to be honest. I just can't seem to get my front leg high enough.

Coach Wyatt thinks it's a physical thing, but I know

it's all in my head. I tripped on a hurdle as a young runner. Badly. I chipped a bone in my elbow and spent six weeks with my arm in a sling. It hurt like crazy. The pain is seared into my memory, and I wonder if I'll ever get over my fear of hurdling.

The time on my GPS band reads 9:26. Still over two and a half hours of game time remain.

A flash of color catches my eye. It's Damon, and he's running straight toward me. "Get out of here!" he yells. "Miss Frost is coming!"

☆☆☆

I turn and run, joining Damon in a frantic scramble. We sidestep trees, weaving our way through the woods. I can hear Miss Frost gaining on us. She's some athlete.

We burst into a clearing, panting for breath, and stop dead in our tracks. The river is straight ahead—it's wound around and cut us off. There are dozens of large boulders on the right, thick forest on the left.

Having the same idea, we take off to the left, but Damon's clumsy strides clip my heel. I trip and face plant into the ground.

Damon slips through a gap in the forest and vanishes from sight.

Light footsteps reach the clearing, and I look up to see Miss Frost standing about ten yards away. "Well, well, well," she says quietly. She's not even breathing hard. "I wasn't expecting Damien to lead me to the famous Milly Amsterdam."

"Please," I beg, thinking of Scarlett. "I don't care that you get our names wrong. Just give me another chance."

Miss Frost laughs. It's a surprisingly musical laugh, the type you would expect to hear at a dinner party or in a conversation with friends. Then her voice returns to a murderous whisper. "You must have rocks in your head if you think I'd give you a second chance." She glances at her GPS tracker and then left at the forest. "This is far too easy. I should have given myself less time—"

But I've leapt up and ducked behind one of the boulders to the right. I scan the landscape frantically. There's an opening between two more boulders farther back, and I squeeze through them. I'm not going down without a fight.

Miss Frost's whisper seeps through the stone. "I can see you on my tracker, Mildred."

I edge back silently, moving farther into the labyrinth. My shoulder brushes against something yellow. It's a flower loose on the stone, just like the flowers in my headband. I grab it and press farther into the maze, flattening my stomach to fit between two more boulders.

The ground starts to slant away. I drop to my haunches and follow the slope, sliding under a gap in the rocks. I almost put my hand down on another yellow flower but see it just in time. I add it to the growing collection in my headband and continue crawling forward.

"You *do* make the chase more fun," a whisper teases.

It floats through the space between the rocks behind me. "If only Alfred had put up such a fight. The silly child curled into a pitiful ball when I found him. But you, Misty...*you* turn the hunt into sport."

There's a small cave carved into the base of one of the boulders. A blue feather lies at the entrance. I roll into the crevice, clutching the plume.

"The signal has dropped out." The whisper is frustrated. "Where did she go?"

I press myself flat against the base of the cold rock, as far into the hollow as I can.

Miss Frost's white sneakers suddenly fill the narrow entrance of the cave, blocking the light. She's so close, I can see the pattern in her silver laces. "I know you're around here somewhere," she says. I can hear her tapping the tracker. "Work, you blasted thing."

I hold my breath, tensing every muscle in my body. My fingers squeeze the quill of the feather.

The shoes shuffle on the leaf litter. I can read the

branding on the side, and I pray she doesn't kick me in the face. "She can't have gotten far."

I shut my eyes, too terrified to watch. If Miss Frost looks down, she'll see where I'm hiding. Then all she'd have to do is reach in and tag me. There's no escape.

"Perhaps she went through that gap," she mutters to herself.

I pray it's not the gap I'm hiding in.

Please don't look down. Please don't look down.

The shoes take two slow steps and stop again. I can hear Miss Frost pressing buttons on the tracker.

I dare not exhale.

"I will find you, Minty," she whispers, "if it's the last thing I do." With that, her shoes leap onto a rock, and she strides away.

I bump into Evie at the edge of the river. She's cowering behind a shrub, sobbing uncontrollably.

"Evie," I say, "are you okay?"

She shakes her head. "I'm so scared. I don't want Miss Frost to find me."

I squat down and put my arm around her. "I'm scared too," I say. "But you need to keep moving. You'll be an easy target if you stay in one spot."

"She hasn't found me yet," says Evie stubbornly. Fear has made her defiant.

I rub her back. "You *must* keep moving. I know how brave you can be," I say. "I really do."

Evie looks at me with uncertain eyes. "Truly?"

I squeeze her shoulder. "I'll never forget the story you told us in class. You know, the one about the washing machine. I wish *I* was that brave."

Evie smiles, and her body relaxes.

"Do you know if anyone else has been caught?" I ask. "I know Myra, Albert, Harold, and Victoria are back at camp."

Evie's smile fades. "I saw her chase down Ren and Vinnie." She pauses and stares into space. "And Sammy."

"Sammy!?" I blurt.

Evie nods. "I saw it all. She hunted him down like a cheetah chasing its prey. She moves like lightning."

This is bad news. Sammy is almost as fast as me. I wonder if my fastest sprint will be enough to escape when I need to.

The edge of the river laps the bank. I check the time on my band: 10:12. "I need to get going," I say. "There are some trees farther down the river. I'm going to check them out. I really don't think you should stay here."

Evie pulls her knees to her chest and shakes her head. "I'm not moving."

"Your call," I say. "But I know you have it in you." I give Evie another squeeze and stand to leave.

I move under the cover of the steep embankment and follow the river for a while. There is a cluster of tall pine trees ahead—a vantage point.

Pine trees are a cinch to climb. We have one in our backyard. Coach Wyatt tells me to climb it as often as I can for training. He says it's good for my agility. He says it will build up strength in my legs and improve my hurdling. If only it took away my fear of tripping.

The pine trees at the river are great for climbing. I take hold of the lowest branch and hurl myself up. I secure my footing on the next branch and ascend higher. I already have a much better view of the surrounding area. I climb a few more rungs and survey the landscape in more detail.

There is a dirt road to the north of the embankment. It leads to a bridge in one direction and the main campsite in the other. I can just make out the tiny figures of those who have been caught, sitting around the smoky fire. I don't have much room to play with. The road is a boundary that, together with the river, forms a corner in the field of play and limits my options. I need to return to the ground and escape from the junction.

"Miffy!"

There's a scream from the direction I've just come. It's Evie.

I hold tightly to the branch and watch as Evie, chased by Miss Frost, scurries along the river's edge toward the pine trees. She's leading the hunter directly to me. I want to call out

for her to stop. I want to tell her to run in a different direction. But yelling would give me away.

My sweaty hands grip the pine, and I clamber up about a dozen branches. Then I spot something strangely familiar. There is a yellow flower on the next branch and two more on the branches beyond. They form a floral trail leading farther up the tree.

The trail leads to a blue feather exactly like the two I found earlier. I scramble to the branch with the feather and take hold of it.

Evie is at the base of the tree. She's desperately peering up through the branches, trying to find me. "Help me!"

Miss Frost leaps out and tags her. "Got you!"

I squash myself against the middle of the tree, hoping it's enough to hide me from view. Hoping Miss Frost doesn't look up.

"Miffy," pleads Evie. "Help!"

"What are you talking about?" says Miss Frost.

"Skippy is nowhere in the vicinity. Look." She points to her tracker. "See? Now, give me your band."

Evie trembles as she passes her band to the teacher.

"You can join Brayman back at camp," says Miss Frost. "I found him not two minutes ago."

Brayman?

Brayman...

Damon! Miss Frost must have found Damon.

That leaves only me, Slugger, Carrot, and...

"Scarlett!" cries Evie. She's caught sight of her friend's red ribbon by the river, and in her anxiety, she has given her away.

Miss Frost turns swiftly and rushes toward Scarlett. She's tagged in the blink of an eye and joins Evie in a despondent walk back to camp.

I try to see where Miss Frost is, but she's vanished into the surrounding scrub as quickly as she appeared. Once again, she's taken off without seeing me.

Why? Why can't she see me on her tracker? Is it

something about the yellow flowers and blue feathers? Every time I find them, Miss Frost seems to lose me.

I study the blue feather in my hand. I reach up to my headband and pull the other feathers loose. The way the sunlight makes them shimmer reminds me of something. Suddenly, it becomes crystal clear, like clouds dissolving away.

The feathers belong to Dodger.

☆ ☆ ☆

11:37.

There is under half an hour of time remaining, and it's come down to me, Slugger, and Carrot. Three players left to determine Scarlett's fate.

I climb down the pine tree and head toward the main campsite. I figure it's the last place Miss Frost would expect me to go. Plus, if I show up on her tracker, there are plenty of options for a getaway.

Using the cover of some prickly bushes, I creep

closer. My ears are working in overdrive, listening out for anything that might be Miss Frost.

My classmates are sitting on the logs beneath the twisted gum tree. It looks like they're writing in books, but at least they seem to be happier now that they're back with Mr. Bambuckle.

Just as I'm about to edge closer, Slugger lumbers into view. He shakes his head as he enters the campsite. I look at his wrist and notice that he's not wearing a band. He's been caught!

It's just me and Carrot. Unless…

I peer out from behind the bushes and scan the campsite for Carrot. There's no sign of him. I sigh with relief.

Slugger slumps down on a log. It cracks under his weight. I don't think I've ever seen him this dejected.

Mr. Bambuckle spots Slugger and walks over to him. He hands him a drink, and Slugger musters a smile. He points back to the way he came and acts out a pushing motion. He's telling the teacher something, and it looks important. Mr. Bambuckle nods as he listens.

The teacher signals to Evie, who brings a notebook over to Slugger.

The rest of the class are busy writing. Mr. Bambuckle has found a distraction to put them at ease. Even Scarlett seems too occupied by her work to be worried. Victoria stands up to stretch and looks in my direction. I duck behind the safety of the bush before I can be seen.

But I have been seen.

Miss Frost is leaning against a tree behind me. She looks like she's been standing there for a while, relishing the moment. She smiles cruelly and presses a button on her tracking device. "There are but two signals left," she says. "I shall enjoy catching you and Garret."

In my desperation to get away, my foot slides on loose dirt, and I graze my knee. "You'll *never* catch me!" I cry.

The commotion draws the attention of my class-mates. I can hear them calling as I sprint away.

"There's Miffy!"

"Run!"

"Go, Miffy!"

"She's right behind you!"

"Watch out for that rock!"

I dare not turn around, putting all my energy into navigating what's in front of me. I sidestep the rock and tear into clear space. Pure adrenaline pumps through my veins.

Miss Frost is close behind. I can hear her footsteps, light and fast. Carrot will be no match for her, so I have to hold her off for as long as possible.

I leap over low-lying ferns and push toward the thick forest. I may be able to lose her there.

Miss Frost surges to the right and angles me away from the trees. She starts herding me back to the river where it's more open.

A thin tree looms. I leap toward it and grab the smooth trunk with my hands. I spin sideways and shoot out at ninety degrees to the right. Miss Frost nearly slips over trying to turn with me. I gain precious seconds and beat her to the forest.

I zigzag between the trees at top speed. If I can get far enough into the forest, Miss Frost will lose visual, and she'll have to rely on her tracker.

I remember the yellow flowers and keep my eyes peeled.

I skirt along the edge of a small gully and cut deeper into the trees. The terrain is becoming rough, and there are fallen logs everywhere.

The *whoosh* and *crunch* of trampled foliage behind me are getting louder. I dare a backward glance, and I'm shocked at how close Miss Frost is. She eases into the picture, her gray-blue eyes burning holes in mine.

My glance is costly. I trip on a rock and tumble forward, rolling head over heels and crashing to a complete stop.

Miss Frost slows to a halt. She stands over me and gloats. "Is that all you've got, Minnie?"

"No!" I cry, and I dive between her legs, rolling out the other side. I'm up and sprinting away before she has time to blink.

☆☆☆

Miss Frost is gaining again. I lead her farther into the forest, desperately trying to lose her among the trees.

There's no sign of any yellow flowers. No blue feathers. I muster my reserve energy and push for a second wind. Coach Wyatt would be yelling at me to keep going.

Miss Frost is getting closer and closer. I can hear her breathing behind me. An icy wind touches my neck.

A fallen log blocks my path. I have a sudden flashback to my failed hurdles race. I remember Coach Wyatt screaming at me to raise my front leg. I remember the sting of falling. I remember the stab of pain in my elbow.

I grit my teeth and run full steam at the log. I can't help but think of the wink Mr. Bambuckle gave me when Miss Frost was explaining the challenge. Did he know this moment was coming? I launch toward the log and clear it with my leading foot. My back toe brushes the bark, but I've made it!

There are more fallen tree trunks ahead, and I run at them with renewed confidence. I time my leaps and raise my front leg high enough to clear each one with perfection.

Miss Frost stumbles at the logs and loses ground. It buys me enough time to loop around and start heading back toward the main campsite.

My muscles are beginning to burn, but I push on as hard as I can. I think of Scarlett and whatever awful punishment Miss Frost has planned. I can't let her catch me. I have to hold her off to give Carrot the best chance of winning.

11:51.

I tear between the trees, dodging low branches and bounding over rocks and shrubs. My legs power on their reserve energy, pumping, working, running.

Miss Frost has regained some lost ground, and there

is a real urgency in her steps. She's breathing heavily now, and I know she means business.

The campsite comes into view, and I race toward it. My classmates have spotted me again and voice their support.

"Keep going, Miffy!"

"You can do it!"

"She's getting closer!"

11:53.

I turn toward the river.

"Nooo!"

The cries from camp tell me I am tagged before I feel Miss Frost's hand on my shoulder. I collapse to the ground, out of breath, out of hope, and out of the game.

Miss Frost is panting. "Quick, give me your band." She examines the tracking device. "Only one signal left."

It's 11:54 when I pass my band to Miss Frost. She hastily pockets it and is off in a flash.

I want to sob for Carrot, though there's no air in

my lungs even for that. I am spent both physically and emotionally.

Sammy runs over and helps me up. "You did everything you could, Miffy," he says. "It's okay. Carrot's still in the game." His words are kind, though I can sense in his voice he knows our classmate will be caught.

He walks me back to camp, and I crumple in a heap.

☆ ☆ ☆

Mr. Bambuckle hands me a cup of water. "You did a terrific thing, dear Miffy."

"But I got caught," I say, taking the cup. "I lost."

The teacher's smile is understanding and optimistic. "Far from it. You'd be surprised what an athlete like yourself is capable of."

"What do you mean?" I say.

Mr. Bambuckle looks at me intently. "Dearest Miffy, I don't know anyone else who could have bought Carrot the time you did."

"But she's too fast," I say. "Carrot doesn't stand a chance."

"Quite the opposite! If my calculations are correct—and I had dear Albert double-check this—Miss Frost will be returning with the victorious Carrot just about...now!"

I turn to see my orange-haired classmate step into the campsite, accompanied by Miss Frost. His face is beaming. I haven't seen him smile like this since the drone race. "We won!" he says. "Scarlett is safe from punishment." He points to his GPS band, which reads 12:03.

Carrot is swamped by my classmates. They lift him onto their shoulders and shout in celebration.

Sammy high-fives Carrot. "You of all people. Amazing. How did you do it?"

Carrot's hair

glows. "I dunno. Just a little bit of luck, I suppose. Though I nearly got caught. Miss Frost was charging at me earlier in the game, and Slugger, who happened to be with me, pushed me into the safety of a small ravine. I wasn't tagged, and it was the perfect hiding place, so I stayed there. By the time I was tracked down, it was too late."

Miss Frost sizes up Scarlett with a terrifying stare and marches away to her car.

"You, dear Miffy," says Mr. Bambuckle, "are an asset to any team, be it club or state level." He pats me on the shoulder. "I'm most certain Coach Wyatt will be thrilled to receive the footage of your bush hurdling."

Dodger flutters over and drops a tiny camera into my lap.

"He filmed the whole thing," says Mr. Bambuckle. "Your coach will be most impressed."

The blue jay's plumes remind me of something. I take the feathers out of my headband and pass them to Mr. Bambuckle. "These are Dodger's, aren't they?" I say.

Mr. Bambuckle's green eyes flash with cheekiness. "Ah, yes. I see Peter's and Dodger's hard work paid off. I had them leave little trails for you here and there. Dodger used his feathers to map important places around the campsite, and Peter set out the flowers last night."

"What were they for?" I ask. "Why did the flowers lead to Dodger's feathers?"

"GPS black spots, of course," says Mr. Bambuckle. "Dodger selected this campsite especially for it. He marked out safe havens where you couldn't be tracked."

Harold is in awe. "The GPS dreadlocks."

Mr. Bambuckle grins. "Just between you and me," he says, "Miss Frost should know all too well that technology can be a curious thing."

6

The Snow Crocus

Miss Frost came down hard on the children after lunch. She didn't like being beaten, and she was determined to make their lives miserable. "You shall spend the entire afternoon writing a reflection about the importance of physical activity. I expect at least five hundred words, fluent and legible. If there are any errors—even just one—you will write the entire thing again."

Vinnie raised a tentative hand.

"Yes, Vanessa?"

"I've already written a reflection," said Vinnie. "I wrote it while we were waiting for the challenge to finish. Mr. Bambuckle told us to—"

"Show me," snapped the assistant principal.

Vinnie handed Miss Frost her two pages of carefully constructed writing. The teacher's lips fidgeted as they often did when she was unable to find fault. "And what about the rest of you?"

The rest of the class, led by the much-relieved Scarlett, took their work to the teacher, whose lips now convulsed in agitated bursts. Even Miffy had managed to record a detailed reflection in the short time it took to eat lunch. She had been taught well by Mr. Bambuckle and was only too happy to show off her writing chops.

Miss Frost clutched the sheets of paper in despair, her pride taking another hard blow. Even though she held all the cards, she felt as though her hand was constantly being trumped by this class of misfits and their bumbling teacher. In pure bitterness, she allowed a dark cloud to enter her mind.

Then Scarlett approached Miss Frost and did something unthinkable. She wrapped her arms around the

teacher and squeezed her waist in a hug bearing uncon-
ditional forgiveness. "Miss Frost, I would like to thank
you for giving me another chance. I promise I will try my
best to meet your expectations." She squeezed
tighter, adding, "And I'll try not to zap you
to any exotic locations again."

The students giggled. It was one of
those soft ripples of laughter that carried
the perfect blend of fondness and
relief. Perhaps the assistant principal would turn a corner.

The lovely gesture, however,
was not well received. Miss
Frost glowered at Scarlett
with renewed coldness. How
could a child like this get the better
of her? How dare she promise to
change when she had committed such a heinous act just
weeks before? This was the last straw. The dark cloud in

Miss Frost's mind triggered an icy decision, shattering the promise she had made earlier that day.

"I need to make a phone call," she said suddenly.

"Oh," said Scarlett, loosening her grip so Miss Frost could step away.

The teacher pulled out her phone and selected a number.

"Who's she calling?" whispered Myra.

Miss Frost heard Myra's question and moved farther away from them with a sneer. She was playing a new game, and the students didn't like it one little bit.

Mr. Bambuckle, meanwhile, caught Scarlett's eye and gave her an affirming nod. "Your forgiveness is a marvelous thing, dear child. When you draw on such strength, you can thrive in even the harshest conditions."

Scarlett smiled. "Thanks, Mr. Bambuckle."

Miss Frost was now speaking quietly on the phone, and Harold dared inch closer to where she was standing. "She's saying something about hair gel," he said.

"Hair gel?" said Albert. "What could she possibly want with hair gel?"

"Wait a moment," said Harold. "I think I'm wrong. She's saying something about ex-bells."

"Ex-bells?" said Albert. "That's stranger still."

Harold took another step closer to Miss Frost. "Wrong again. It's something about someone being repelled. Or egg spelled."

Albert glanced at Scarlett. "She couldn't mean *expelled*, could she?"

Miss Frost sensed the class was catching on, and she waltzed cruelly within earshot.

"Mr. Geeves, I understand your shock. I am expelling her due to unreasonable behavior at school… Yes, I am quite serious… It was a computer program called PhotoCrop… Mr. Geeves, do I sound like I'm joking? I shall send you a text message with the address of the camp, and you and Mrs. Geeves are to come and collect Charlotte—sorry, yes, Scarlett—immediately. Goodbye."

Miss Frost tucked her phone back into her pocket and turned to the class. "My expectations *will* be met. Discipline is the new order." She straightened her top and turned toward her car. "Skylight, you have half an hour to pack your things. I'm off to complete some paperwork."

As Miss Frost walked away, the gravity of her decision hit the students like a ton of bricks. Ren and Vinnie embraced the shell-shocked Scarlett, Carrot's eyes watered uncontrollably, and Evie curled up into a tiny ball at Victoria's feet.

Although Mr. Bambuckle knew this wasn't the end of the story, he understood this was a low point, so he asked the students to gather around.

"She promised there would be no punishment," managed Scarlett, wiping away a tear.

"Why is Miss Frost so mean?" said Miffy, who felt as though her effort during the game had been wasted.

Mr. Bambuckle offered a reassuring smile, pausing to ensure Scarlett was drawn in by its comfort. "Dear children, as difficult as this is, I must *urge* you to take heart and follow Scarlett's strength. We would be foolish to forget the example of the snow crocus."

"The snow crocodile?" said Harold. "There's no such thing."

"Not crocodile, dear Harold," said the teacher. "Crocus."

"What's a snow crocus?" asked Ren.

"Oh, pick me!" said Albert, who had read about crocuses in books.

Mr. Bambuckle retrieved his frying pan from one of his pockets and flipped it in the air. It spun twice, and he caught it with the ease of a seasoned juggler. "Kindly tell us what you know, dear boy."

Albert adjusted his glasses. "The snow crocus is a flower that's known to bloom in cold conditions. It can even burst into color through snow."

"Your knowledge is a beautiful thing," said Mr. Bambuckle.

"I know a beautiful thing," said Damon, gazing at Victoria.

Mr. Bambuckle flipped the pan, which was now sizzling, again and caught it with his other hand.

"I detect the aroma of pancakes," said Slugger.

"Right you are," said Mr. Bambuckle with a smile. "There is so much wonderful knowledge in this group. I must never take it for granted."

Miffy scratched her head. "I'm confused. What do snow crocuses have to do with Scarlett and Miss Frost?"

Mr. Bambuckle's green eyes shone. As someone who welcomed curiosity, he knew the question warranted a thoughtful response. "Just like the snow crocus can blossom through the ice, people can flourish in difficult times. The snow crocus is indeed a special flower. It often represents the end of winter and the early stages of spring. Scarlett demonstrated this marvelous strength when she hugged Miss Frost. I have no doubt she will continue being courageous for a long time to come."

"Are you saying Scarlett will be okay, even if Miss Frost has just expelled her?" said Miffy.

"Of that, I am most certain," said Mr. Bambuckle. "And perhaps even Miss Frost will someday bloom. I sense her winter will eventually come to an end."

There was a moment's silence as the students thought about what their teacher had explained. Knowing full well there was truth to everything he said, their miserable thoughts for Scarlett turned to hope.

The color returned to Scarlett's cheeks, and she stood up. "I think I have the strength to pack my things now."

"I *know* you have the strength to do so," said the teacher.

Scarlett let the comment sink in, then walked to her tent.

Mr. Bambuckle whistled, tossing his frying pan into the air once more. This time, he caught it behind his back.

The students watched in admiration for quite some time, marveling at their teacher's skill.

"Why do you keep flipping the *pan*?" asked Harold eventually.

"Because flipping *pancakes* is too easy," said Mr. Bambuckle. "And I do believe they're ready. Who would like one?"

"Me, please!" sang a chorus of voices.

As the students reached for the tasty snacks, Scarlett returned with her belongings.

Although the students were now feeling much better about things, their uncertainty for their classmate's future added a somber tone to the afternoon.

Harold offered Scarlett his pancake. "We believe in you," he said. "We know you are remarkable. Even though you have to leave our school, we have faith you will be okay, because you're strong."

Scarlett smiled. "It's *you* who make me strong," she said, addressing the entire class, including Mr. Bambuckle.

"But it's *you* who blossoms," said Harold. "You're a snow crocodile."

Scarlett managed a laugh. "Before I go, I have one thing to ask."

"Ask you may," said Mr. Bambuckle.

"I've never been in a class like this before," said Scarlett, "and I've never had a teacher like you, Mr. Bambuckle. Could we please do one last fun activity before my parents arrive?"

Mr. Bambuckle's chest filled with pride. His pupil was already demonstrating the positivity she needed to see this day through. "You name it, dear Scarlett."

"I've always loved your creative lessons," she said.

"Can we do one of those? What about ridiculous uses for a stick?"

"A stick it is," said Mr. Bambuckle. "Brainstorm away."

Fifteen Ridiculous Uses for a Stick

1) Use it to pick your nose. Then eat it. The stick, that is, not the snot!

2) Use it to pick someone else's nose. They'll be thankful for the unblocked airways. Don't forget to eat it. The snot, that is, not the airways. People need those to breathe.

3) Balance it over your top lip and sport a woody moustache.

4) Keep it as your best friend. Sticks are awesome because they never complain.

5) Decorate it with romantic song lyrics and give it to Victoria Goldenhorn.

6) Sticks and bones may break my stones... No, that's not it. Stones and flicks may break my rocks, but names... No, that's not it. Sticks and crows may make a toe... Hmmm, something is not quite working out here. Sticks and stones may break my bones, but names will only cause self-doubt and insecurity. Yes, that's it!

7) Dip it in ink and use it as a stylish, rustic pen.

8) Use it as an improvised fishing pole. You'll need a line as well—a shoelace should do the trick. As for the bait, use caramel donuts.

9) Use the stick to unstick a stack of stuck stockings in a steep street.

10) Collect 5,256 sticks and use them to build a house. Note: don't invite a big bad wolf over for dinner. He'll huff and he'll puff—not to blow the house down, but because he's awfully unfit. He should have listened to Coach Wyatt.

11) Use it as a drumstick! Use your annoying little sister's head as the drum. Nah, that's just mean. Your parents shouldn't have to put up with the noise.

12) Use it for puns—if you're prepared to branch out a little. Stick with it, and you'll see what I mean. I'm sure you'll twig on it. Get out of here. Leaf if you can't think of any ideas. Just don't expect a pat on the bark.

13) Use it to play fetch with your pet dog. Let the dog throw the stick, then run after it and pick it up with your teeth. Your dog will pat you on the head and wrestle the stick out of your mouth and throw it again for you. If you're good, you may even get a steak for dinner.

14) Make it into a giant sliver. Ouch!
15) Sell it on a gum tree. Not the website, silly. Climb a gum tree and sell it up there.

7

Teamwork Charades

As it turned out, the students had time for a second wonderful lesson. The afternoon sun was dipping on the horizon, and Scarlett's parents were yet to arrive. So Mr. Bambuckle improvised under the watchful eye of Miss Frost, who had finished her paperwork and returned to the main campsite.

"Dear children, now is a splendid time for a game of teamwork charades," said the teacher.

"Is it the same as normal charades?" asked Damon.

"Indeed. Though you'll be working with a partner."

Miss Frost was taking notes. She was recording

everything the teacher did and would be giving a full report to Mr. Sternblast at the conclusion of camp.

Mr. Bambuckle gestured for Ren and Vinnie to stand up. "I'd be delighted if you two would kick things off for us."

The best friends had a secretive discussion before turning to face their classmates. Vinnie pressed her hands together and then unfolded them.

"Book," said Albert.

Vinnie nodded.

Ren held up two fingers.

"Two words," said Albert.

"Give someone else a chance, brainiac," said Slugger.

"Sorry," said Albert.

Vinnie held up a single finger.

"What's that!?" cried Slugger.

"She wants us to guess the first word," said Albert.

"Oh."

Vinnie grabbed a bunch of her hair and waved it around.

"Hair?"

"Brown?"

"Curls?"

"Hairy?"

Vinnie nodded.

"Okay, hairy."

Ren held up two fingers.

"Peace," said Slugger.

Albert shook his head. "She's not making the peace sign. She's telling us this is the second word."

"Ooh, gotcha."

Ren acted out going to the toilet.

"Bathroom?"

"Lavatory?"

"Potty?"

Ren nodded.

"Hairy and potty."

"Hairy Potty?"

"Oh, Harry Potter!"

Vinnie and Ren burst out laughing. "Yes!"

Damon and Evie were next to have a turn. Evie rolled her arm forward, motioning an old-fashioned camera.

"Movie!"

Damon held up one finger and pointed to Miss Frost.

"*Frozen!*" said Myra. "That was too easy."

"Very funny," whispered Miss Frost. She was clearly unimpressed with the proceedings. "I'm not sure what you think the benefits of this nonsensical game are," she added, directing a stare at Mr. Bambuckle.

Mr. Bambuckle chuckled. "It's a most wonderful activity, Miss Frost. You'll find outcomes CM13-C, TM4-A, and PD5-B have been fully covered in just five minutes."

Miss Frost flicked through her notes. "This is absurd. What sort of teacher ticks off outcomes with tomfoolery like this?"

"Let me ask you this instead," said Mr. Bambuckle. "What sort of adults do we want our students to become?

You'll find the outcomes covered include communication, teamwork, and persistence…if you're having trouble finding them, that is."

Miss Frost tightened her lips. She knew the teacher was right. "Go on then," she said. "You may continue to *play*."

Slugger and Carrot were up next, the latter indicating the pair would be acting out another film.

"Two words."

Carrot held up a single finger.

"First word."

The orange-haired boy pointed to the sky and wiggled his fingers delicately.

"Stars?"

"Star?"

Carrot nodded, satisfied with his well-executed mime.

Slugger held up two fingers.

"Second word."

The hulking food enthusiast pretended to attack. He raised his arms and grabbed hold of Carrot's shoulders. Carrot retaliated by throwing a slow-motion punch, which Slugger ducked.

Victoria giggled.

Slugger then threw a slow-motion punch of his own. Carrot swayed backward to the chuckles of his classmates. Slugger followed up with a clumsy roundhouse kick, which made him lose his balance. He toppled over and landed on Carrot, who had unfortunately mistimed his evasive roll.

"Amazing fight sequence," squealed Myra. "Wars! It's *Star Wars*!"

Carrot raised a thumb from somewhere underneath Slugger.

The class burst out laughing, and the boys stood up, though not before a pair of particularly sharp scissors fell from one of Slugger's pockets.

Miss Frost glanced between the scissors and Mr.

Bambuckle. "Those are clearly not school-regulated scissors," she said. "How interesting. A teacher permitting students to carry dangerous items at camp."

Slugger stared at the scissors on the ground. "You don't understand. I—"

"Quiet," said Miss Frost. She shot a fierce look

toward Mr. Bambuckle, clearly more concerned with the impact this could have on him.

The assistant principal scribbled in her folder. This incident, she knew, was the perfect ammunition for Mr. Sternblast. She stood up abruptly. "I must report this at once. I'll be in my car if anyone needs me."

Slugger furrowed his brows and turned to Mr. Bambuckle, ashamed the scissors had caused such a commotion. "I'm sorry. I didn't mean for that to happen."

Mr. Bambuckle's blue jacket twinkled in the afternoon light. "I believe you have some explaining to do," said the kindly teacher. "Now is the time to be honest."

The Hit-Man Hairdresser
Slugger Choppers's Story

Someone planted the scissors in my pocket. I don't know anything about them.

Come on, Slugger. Tell the truth.

The devil made me do it. He forced me to put the scissors in my pocket against my will.

Mr. Bambuckle can tell you're not being honest, Slugger.

The scissors actually fell out of Carrot's pocket. It was an optical illusion that made it look like they fell from mine.

Tell the teacher the facts. You can do it.

Okay, okay. I'll be frank. I'm a hit-man hairdresser. I've been trying to chop off Carrot's hair. Vex hired me as part of some sick revenge plan. That's the honest truth.

Finally, it's off my chest. I can breathe easy.

It all started when Vex approached me before we left for camp. He was holding a wad of fifty-dollar bills.

"What are you doing with so much cash?" I asked.

"Shh, keep your voice down," said Vex. "I have a proposal for you."

I was flattered. "Thanks, but I don't particularly want to marry you."

"Not that type of proposal, dimwit," said Vex.

"Oh."

"I want you to take out Carrot Grigson."

"That would be fun," I said. "I love going out to places. It'll be nice to spend some quality time with him, and there's a restaurant I've been dying to try."

Vex rolled his eyes. "Not that sort of taking out. I

mean *taking out* taking out. You know, make it look like an accident."

"You want me to accidentally take Carrot to a restaurant?"

Vex ran an agitated hand through his dark hair. "Are you dumb or something? No, I want you to *get* Carrot. I want you to chop his hair off. I want him to feel the embarrassment I felt before the drone race. Dad's been teaching me the importance of dominance, and I've been biding my time with this plan. Carrot made me lose my hair, and now it's time for him to experience the same humiliation."

"Oh."

"So are you in?" said Vex. He waved the money in front of my face.

"Not for me, thank you very much," I said. "I need to report you to Mr. Sternblast immediately."

Slugger, Slugger, Slugger. Don't drift from the truth.

Sorry, that's not what happened.

"Yeah, I might be interested in a job like that," I said. "How much?"

"Six hundred bucks," said Vex. "I swiped it from my dad's wallet. He won't miss it. You know, three car dealerships and everything. Plus, I figure he owes me even more with all the overtime I've been doing."

I stared at the cash. "Six hundred bucks... That's almost half a thousand."

Vex slapped his forehead. "It's more than that, nincompoop. Half a thousand is *five* hundred. *Six* hundred is sixty percent, which is more than half... Look, I haven't got time for a stupid math lesson. I'm tired enough as it is from working all night at the car dealership. I just need to know...are you in or out?"

"I'm in," I said. "It should be pretty easy to do at camp."

Vex handed me three hundred dollars. "Half now, then half when you chop Carrot's hair."

"What about the other half?" I said.

Vex groaned in annoyance.

"You really want to get him, don't you?" I said.

A dark look flashed across Vex's face. "You don't know the trouble it's caused me, that whole drone debacle. Dad still hasn't forgiven me for getting caught cutting the wires in Carrot's project. An eye for an eye, a haircut for a haircut."

I thumbed through the fifty-dollar bills. "Okay, half now and half later. And half when—"

"There are only two halves!" said Vex. "It's a deal." He slid a pair of sharp scissors into my hands. "You can use these," he added. "Otherwise, feel free to be creative."

☆ ☆ ☆

"I need someone to take the wheel for a moment. Slugger, would you be so kind?"

I have to admit, it was nice to be offered the job of driving the bus. Not many teachers let their students do stuff like that. Mr. Bambuckle puts a lot of faith in us.

Sliding into the driver's seat brought back memories of the day I drove a school bus. The government had made a mistake that meant kids could drive. It was a crazy day!

So on the bus to camp, my driving skills flooded back like…a flood. Sorry, I'm not very good at similes.

Mr. Bambuckle stood at the door. "I have an urgent matter to attend to. Slugger, would you please?" He tapped the glass door.

"Open it?" I said. What on earth was the teacher planning to do?

I tried to play it cool, but there were so many buttons on the dash, and they were all different from the other bus I'd driven. I fumbled around until I hit the right one.

Mr. Bambuckle casually stepped out of the moving vehicle, and everyone started to freak out.

I could see Carrot in the rearview mirror. He was sitting close to an open window on the left-hand side of the bus. With his face pressed up to the glass, some of his hair was poking outside.

I remembered my deal with Vex.

Mr. Bambuckle stepped back onto the bus with Dodger. The blue jay fluttered around for a while, and I noticed my classmates were distracted. It was the perfect opportunity for me to get Carrot. If I drove the bus close enough to something sharp outside, I might have been able to clip off some of his hair.

I veered off the road and lined up the left side of the bus with a huge twisted gum tree. With a little bit of luck, Carrot's hair might snag on the low-hanging branches.

Dodger looped around inside the bus. "He *really* is a beautiful bird," I said, glancing over my shoulder. It was the best I could come up with to make it seem like I was distracted. I had to make it look like an accident.

"He most certainly is," agreed Mr. Bambuckle, speaking of Dodger's beauty. "And Slugger, keep an eye on the road, since you're no longer on it."

"Argh!"

Mr. Bambuckle's voice brought me back to reality. In that split second, his brilliant lessons flashed through my mind. He had taught us to work together and to look out for each other. How could I hurt Carrot? How could I hurt anyone? I slammed my foot on the brake, and we came skidding to a stop just inches from the tree.

"We're very close to those branches," observed Carrot.

Ashamed, I sat in the driver's seat until everyone had unpacked. Then I reversed the bus back onto the road. How could I be so foolish?

"You're not just a talented cook," said Mr. Bambuckle as I joined the others at camp. "Nice maneuver."

Mr. Bambuckle was always encouraging me. I could feel my cheeks flushing from a strange mixture of pride and shame. I wondered if I should give the cash and scissors back to Vex.

☆☆☆

I flicked through the money in the dim light of my tent. I'd never had three hundred dollars before. The fact that it was only half of the payment got my blood pumping.

There is this chef I admire— Rosa Carter. She lives in the city and runs master classes every now and then. I've been dying to go to one. I know she could teach me things in person that I could never learn from a podcast or television show. Plus, it's always nice to meet your heroes.

Her master class courses cost six hundred dollars. It's exactly how much I could earn if I finish the job for Vex.

Thinking about the cooking classes was too much temptation, and I headed to the campfire with renewed vigor. I had a job to do, and do it I would.

"Who would like a marshmallow?" said Mr. Bambuckle.

"Me, please!" said everyone.

"First, you'll need to find something to cook them with," said the teacher.

Before I knew it, everyone was disappearing into the woods. I watched Carrot venture off in a direction of his own, so I stole after him as quietly as I could.

Carrot waded through the woods, searching for his perfect roasting stick in the dark. I hid behind a tree and listened hard, gripping the scissors tightly. I had to let my ears guide me. I couldn't risk being seen.

Carrot was chatting away to himself. "I miss you, Pop. I miss you, Jones. Hope you're having fun whatever you're doing."

He rustled through the undergrowth, picking up sticks and tossing them away. "No good," he said. "Too thin... Hmm, this one's okay."

I crept out from behind the cover of the tree to find higher ground. My plan was to rush past him and slice off as much hair as I could before he had time to realize what had happened. I needed a running start.

Carrot ventured closer to my hiding spot, and I took my chance. I launched myself at full speed, aiming the scissors where I thought the top of his head would be.

But I missed.

I whooshed past his head, the curly orange target still intact, and landed awkwardly on the ground.

Carrot got spooked and ran back to the campfire.

Lucky. I was relieved he didn't come over to investigate—I would have been caught red-handed.

As I picked myself up, the smell of a nearby plant drew my attention. I reached out and felt the flower. Could it really be? It was a plant I had heard a lot about but had never come across before. I pulled the plant from the earth, being sure to dislodge the round base of the stem from the soil, then I pocketed it, eager to get back to the fire.

I looped around the woods and entered camp from a different direction. I couldn't let anyone know I had been near Carrot.

Later that evening, my classmates nominated me as head chef. We were going to cook dinner for ourselves and the teachers. I was excited.

Miffy asked if I would like any help with the preparations.

"Yes," I said. "Scarlett and...*Carrot*. Oh, and Ren and Vinnie can choose dessert."

I had an idea, but I needed a little bit of extra time to make it happen.

My two helpers peeled the vegetables while I cooked the chicken over a makeshift fire. When nobody was watching, I retrieved the plant from my pocket and mashed the bulb into a gloopy paste.

Colchicum autumnale—meadow saffron—a poisonous plant that, when ingested, can lead to hair loss.

I began slicing the chicken and serving it up. I cut a slit in the piece I'd allocated for Carrot and carefully dabbed a tiny amount of the paste inside. Once it was set aside, I could put the finishing touches on the dessert.

Eventually, everything was ready, and I made sure Carrot had his special plate with the poisoned chicken.

Mr. Bambuckle was pleased with our efforts. "This is the most astonishing dinner I have *ever* had the privilege of smelling."

He's always so positive. "Thank you," I said. "Just wait until you taste it."

Secretly, I couldn't wait for Carrot to taste *his*.

"Indeed," said Mr. Bambuckle. Then he did something unthinkable. He knocked Carrot's plate out of his hands, and the chicken splattered all over the ground.

How could it be? Did the teacher know about meadow saffron? Could he smell it? The only thing I knew was that my plan had been foiled.

"How very careless of me, dear Carrot. I'm sincerely sorry," said Mr. Bambuckle.

Something in his eyes told me he knew exactly what he was doing. They sparkled knowingly, and he flicked me a quick glance.

☆ ☆ ☆

I love listening to podcasts. They're a great way to study. I know I'm not the sharpest tool in the shed, and I break a lot of things, but I can still learn. I listen to cooking podcasts almost every day because I want to be a gourmet chef when I'm older.

Before bed, I listened to a podcast called *A Hacker's Guide to Hair Removal*. I had to start planning another hairdressing attack from scratch. I paid close attention to the ideas and took mental notes. I thought about how much I wanted that master class with Rosa Carter and found renewed determination. I would strike again the next day.

I didn't sleep well. Damon woke me up by rolling me over because I was snoring. Then he zipped my tent back up too loudly. I've always been a firm believer that slower zipping is quieter. Damon should have done that.

The next day, during Miss Frost's challenge, I found myself alone with Carrot. I hadn't planned for it to work out that way. It just happened.

After seeing Miss Frost chase down Sammy, I fled in the opposite direction and bumped into Carrot along the way.

"I think we're safe here," he said as we stopped for a break on the edge of a shallow ravine.

"I agree," I said.

It was the perfect opportunity. Carrot was completely unsuspecting and knew nothing of the scissors in my pocket. All I had to do was grab him and cut off his hair using the speed snipping technique I'd heard about in the podcast.

I dipped my hand into my pocket and grasped the scissors. But as I did, Miss Frost exploded out from behind some trees and charged straight at us. She must have latched on to the fact that we were together, an easy double target.

It all happened in slow motion. I had the sudden realization that I could protect Carrot. I just had to nudge him down the ravine and distract Miss Frost. We couldn't let her win. We were a team, and teammates work together.

I glanced between Carrot, the ravine, and the charging Miss Frost.

"You'll be safe down there," I said, pushing him gently on the chest.

He stumbled backward and then rolled down the ravine, vanishing beneath a thick bush. He was out of sight.

Miss Frost pulled up suddenly and examined her tracking device. "That Miley Ampersand is nearby." She looked at me and snarled. "You'll be easy pickings later on, Slogger. I have some *real* sport to catch now."

Then she dashed away in another direction.

I lingered at the top of the ravine for a while, waiting to see if Carrot would reemerge. When he didn't, I felt terrible. Maybe I had hurt him? I hadn't meant to. I was honestly trying to protect him from Miss Frost. I was beginning to feel even guiltier about taking Vex up on his offer.

When I found out later that Carrot was not only safe but had won, I was half-relieved, half-angry, and half-hungry (from all the running). I was torn in three like…two pieces. I'm really not very good at similes or math. But then I realized something. As much as I wanted the master class, I wanted Carrot to be okay more. The right thing to do became as green as grass. Or is it as clear as glass? Anyway, the main point is I knew I had to call the deal off. Carrot was more important than the master class with Rosa Carter. I had to learn to put other people before myself.

I went over to Vex's tent and slipped the money through a little gap in the zipper. I didn't want to wake him, but I knew that when he found the money, he'd realize the deal was off.

Which leads me to now and our game of teamwork charades.

The scissors fell out of my pocket because I was stupid and forgot to return them to Vex with the money. I guess I was even more stupid to agree to cut Carrot's hair in the first place.

I'm sorry, Mr. Bambuckle.

I'm sorry, Carrot.

But let me know if you'd ever like a haircut. I know some great techniques.

8

Packing Up

Mr. Bambuckle listened attentively to Slugger's story. The rest of the class looked on too, intrigued as to how the teacher would respond. Carrot in particular, who had no idea of Slugger's intent until now, was utterly absorbed.

"Well, dear Slugger," said Mr. Bambuckle eventually, "I commend you for having the courage to tell me the truth. Honesty is always the first step in being true to yourself."

Slugger sighed with relief.

"However," said the teacher, "we must consider the consequences."

Slugger's head drooped. A punishment, he could handle. His favorite teacher dealing it out, not so much.

Mr. Bambuckle signaled for Carrot to stand. "Slugger, examine your classmate."

"What do you mean?" said Slugger.

"Look at him," said Mr. Bambuckle. "Study him."

"Ummm...okay."

Mr. Bambuckle stood behind Carrot. "Slugger, what do you see?"

Slugger thought about this for a while. "I see Carrot Grigson. I see my friend."

"That is all," said Mr. Bambuckle.

"Wait," said Slugger. "You're not going to punish me?"

Mr. Bambuckle's blue jacket shimmered in the afternoon light. "My dear boy, you've already punished yourself. Anyone who wrestles with right and wrong like you have has experienced quite enough anguish as it is. I'll leave it up to you to continue moving forward."

Slugger nodded slowly, glowing with the confidence his teacher had instilled in him.

"There is just one other matter concerning the situation," said Mr. Bambuckle. "When the time comes, I shall speak to Vex regarding his role in the story."

"Hey! Where did Scarlett go?" said Miffy suddenly.

"She was here a few minutes ago," said Victoria.

"I see brake lights farther down the road," said Sammy. "I think she's gone."

"She *has* gone," said Miss Frost, who had returned to the campfire.

The students had been so engrossed in Slugger's story, they had failed to notice Miss Frost tap Scarlett on the shoulder and lead her away from the campsite. Scarlett had wanted to call out to Mr. Bambuckle and her classmates, but she could not find the right words or bear to interrupt Slugger's story. She was sent away without a farewell or any kind wishes, expelled from Blue Valley School.

Unlike his pupils, Mr. Bambuckle had in fact noticed his beloved student leave. While he had longed to reassure Scarlett that things would work out in the end, he trusted in the girl's resilience. He knew she could survive at any other school, and he looked forward to the day he would welcome her back to Blue Valley.

Miss Frost, meanwhile, took full control of camp. Her position allowed her to dictate terms, and she was using this power to stamp her authority over Mr. Bambuckle. Discipline was the new order.

The rest of the afternoon and evening was a disappointment to the students. The assistant principal made them memorize math problems and spelling words, stopping only for a quick dinner break before working them long into the night.

The children eventually went to bed feeling rather sorry for themselves.

The morning sun broke over the horizon, illuminating the dew on the tents. Damon rolled over in his sleeping bag. He'd slept like a baby, courtesy of the Himalayan tea Mr. Bambuckle had brewed for him before bed.

Slugger had slept like a baby too. He sucked on his thumb through the night, deep in subconscious reflection.

Roused by the brightening sky, the students emerged from their tents and yawned.

Miss Frost greeted them with the snap of a clipboard. "Right, see to it that you pack up everything before breakfast. Ensure your tents are folded correctly."

The children, not wanting any more drama, obeyed robotically. This was how things had been done before Mr. Bambuckle had arrived at Blue Valley School, and it appeared they were fast headed back that way.

"Hey," said Damon, "look what I found!" He sheepishly handed Mr. Bambuckle the pole he had lost while trying to set up the teacher's spare tent.

"No speaking!" hissed Miss Frost.

As the students set about packing up their things, Miss Frost pulled Mr. Bambuckle aside.

"We'll be reporting to Mr. Sternblast immediately upon our return to school. There is, of course, the issue regarding Chugger's dangerous scissors to discuss. You must answer for a violation of section J in the student safety document."

Mr. Bambuckle chuckled. "I'd be delighted to spend the time with you."

The teacher watched as Slugger helped Carrot pull down his tent. Carrot tripped over a tent peg, and Slugger caught him just before he hit the ground. The boys laughed, and Slugger patted Carrot on the back. He then muscled his friend's tent neatly into its bag before attending to his own.

"Look at that," said Mr. Bambuckle. "I believe you'll find outcome RF4-A says a thing or two about taking action after reflecting. It seems Slugger has done both just splendidly."

Miss Frost's lips twitched.

A shadow passed overhead.

"What was that?" said Albert, adjusting his glasses to get a better look.

"I believe the speckled-dagger vulture has decided to make an appearance," said Mr. Bambuckle.

Dodger twittered anxiously from inside one of the teacher's pockets as the shadow passed over them again.

"What utter nonsense," snapped Miss Frost. "It's likely an eagle. There's no such thing as a speckled-dagger vulture. You'll do well to stop filling the children's heads with ridiculous stories."

"And you'll do well to mind yours," said Mr. Bambuckle.

"I beg your pardon?!"

But it was too late. A large blob of bird dropping splashed on top of Miss Frost's silver hair, completely smothering her diamond bobby pin in sticky, smelly yuck.

"Ah, yes," said Mr. Bambuckle. "The speckled-dagger

vulture is rather notorious for doing that."

Miss Frost shrieked and flailed her arms, running away in the direction of her car.

"She looks like one of those inflatable car lot men," said Damon.

"Indeed," said the teacher with a wry smile.

The children hauled their suitcases to the campfire area and sat down. The space left by Scarlett—an empty log—was already felt.

Mr. Bambuckle blinked brightly in the morning sunlight, a knowing look on his face. "I suppose it's time we check on Vex."

"I'll do it," said Sammy, dashing over to his classmate's tent.

The teacher's green eyes glistened like emeralds as

he awaited Sammy's report, and it was only a matter of seconds before the news was broken.

Sammy rushed back to the logs, panting. "He's gone. He's taken his bag and vanished!"

The students gasped.

"He left this note behind," added Sammy, handing a piece of paper to the teacher.

Mr. Bambuckle grinned from ear to ear as he read the note. "It seems Vex has gone on an adventure," he said. "I hope you're all ready for one too." The much-loved teacher's brown hair ruffled in the wind. "I know *I* am."

Don't miss all the laughs with
Mr. Bambuckle and class 12B
in their other adventures!

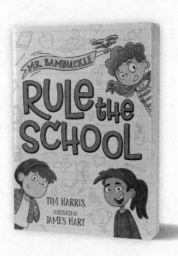

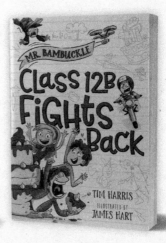